LOVE
ON THE
Main Stage

S.A. DOMINGO

Hodder
Children's
Books

HODDER CHILDREN'S BOOKS

First published in Great Britain in 2020 by Hodder Children's Books

1 3 5 7 9 10 8 6 4 2

Text copyright © S.A. Domingo, 2020

The moral rights of the author have been asserted.

A CIP catalogue record for this book is available from the British Library.

ISBN 978 1 444 95421 0

Typeset in Sabon by Avon DataSet Ltd, Alcester, Warwickshire

Printed and bound in Great Britain by Clays Ltd, Elcograf S.p.A.

The paper and board used in this book
are made from wood from responsible sources.

Hodder Children's Books
An imprint of Hachette Children's Group
Part of Hodder and Stoughton
Carmelite House
50 Victoria Embankment
London EC4Y 0DZ

An Hachette UK Company
www.hachette.co.uk

www.hachettechildrens.co.uk

This book is dedicated to Amy, to Aretha,
to Erykah and Chaka, and all the countless
other incredible musicians who have inspired me!

PART I
Island Rocks

CHAPTER 1

'Five minutes left, please, everyone . . .'

Nova Clarke's eyes roamed over the block of neat handwriting on the page in front of her – and the empty space below it. She'd done her best, but she had a feeling she hadn't exactly aced this exam. She'd given her mate Gemma an exaggerated eye-roll when the girl had actually gestured to the moderator that she had *run out of space* in her answer booklet! Gem had chuckled softly even as she continued her determined scribbling.

Now, as Nova folded her exam paper, she exhaled in relief. Last one! Well, last GCSE anyway

– she fully anticipated years more examinations to come. A levels, and then she knew her mum and dad were expecting her to follow in her brother Otis' footsteps in aiming for that degree neither of her parents had achieved. Not to mention the fact that environmental science, the only field she was *kind of* interested in to getting into, would probably require even more study than that! The gust of another sigh ruffled the pages on the desk in front of her, and Nova grabbed a scrap of paper, subtly jotting down a lyric prompt she planned to add into her notebook later.

Endings and beginnings, ambitions and realities . . .

She knew that environmental scientists didn't usually have a sideline as singer-songwriters, but that job had a bit less 'pipe dream' written all over it, and she really did have a passion for conserving the planet's resources. Besides, just *thinking* about actually sharing her own music and lyrics made her shiver with embarrassment.

'Time!'

A palpable fug of relief lifted off the students in

the hall, and Nova grinned at Gemma. Her friend flopped her head on to the desk dramatically despite clearly having 'flying colours' whipping past her, then sat up and scraped back her chair along with all the other students. They both silently handed in their exam papers before bursting through the doors into the cacophony of noise in the corridor.

'Goodbye, Milton-Lloyd Grammar!' Gem yelled.

'Err, Gemma Aidoo, please keep your ebullience to a minimum,' the moderator, Ms Hartford, called after them, and Gemma rolled her eyes.

'*Ebullience*? Ugh. I cannot wait to ditch this place.'

Nova laughed. 'Babe, it's hardly goodbye, remember. We're going to be back for sixth form in, like, two and a half months?'

'Don't remind me.' Gemma suddenly paused by their lockers, reaching up to place a hand on top of her head. She gestured to Nova to do the same. Gemma's expensive, Beyoncé-inspired wavy auburn weave was pulled back from her face with a conservative navy-blue headband that matched their uniforms. Nova frowned in confusion for a second, then grinned and reached for the elastic hairband that held her own thin dreadlocks back in a neat ponytail.

'Ready? One . . . two . . . three!' Gemma said, and they both whipped their hair free of its confines. '*Who gon' stop me, huh*?' she added through her mirth, quoting B's husband.

Nova only knew that from the umpteen online mixes Gemma had sent her while trying to convince her that hip-hop was better than 'that jazzy, woe-is-me stuff you're always listening to'. But still, she joined in with her friend's relieved laughter. One thing Nova definitely wasn't going to miss over the summer was being told how to wear her hair.

She and Gemma quickly grabbed their bags from their lockers, then linked arms and followed the crowd of their classmates towards the freedom of the open doors at the school's exit. A group of their friends was congregating by the gates, basking in the warm sunshine of early summer, and Nova could already tell they were formulating a plan for post-exam decompression.

'Gemma Aidoo-believe! Super-Nova!' They were greeted by the always-grinning Clive Black, who had fashioned his school tie into a jaunty scarf-arrangement around his neck, and was perched on the wall by the gates. 'So, on a scale of one to ten, *how* painful was that last question?' he enquired as they got closer.

'Bru-tal!' Gemma agreed, as Nova shrugged her own reply.

Then she nudged Gem and chuckled. 'Oh, OK, Ms *Can I get an extra piece of paper*!'

But even after making it all the way to their final GCSEs with her classmates, Nova still felt like a bit of an outsider. Sure, they had all taken the entrance exams to get into their prestigious grammar school, but she was the only one in their group of friends who had a thirty-plus-minute commute to get there. The rest of them were already *expected* to do well, and their postcodes were generally within spitting distance of the school in this leafy, well-off corner of south London. It often felt a world away from Nova's family flat in Brixton, even if her local area was going through its own gentrification.

'Guys, we're heading to the park to eat our body weight in ice cream before Sasha's party tonight,' Tiegen Choi, one of the other girls in the group, announced. 'Nova, Gem, you're in, yeah?'

Nova smiled and was about to respond in the affirmative – an obscenely huge 99 with extra strawberry sauce sounded pretty good right now! But then she spotted an all-too familiar, all-too fun-sapping figure heading in their direction out of the corner of her eye.

'Nate! Yes, mate!' Clive called, launching himself from the wall and jogging over to the approaching tall, handsome boy to smack palms and pull him into a half-hug. Nathan Kahale-Turner, star of their rugby team, and top of their class, second only to Gemma. He was a young Jason Momoa-lookalike – and the boy who was the architect of the giant crack right down the centre of Nova's heart. Two months had hardly been time enough to heal it, that was for certain.

'Coming to the park?' she heard Clive enquire, making her stomach sink.

'Err, yeah, I've just got to hang back for a sec. Mandy forgot something in her locker,' came Nate's reply.

Fan-tastic.

Truth be told, Nova had been constantly surprised by her romantic relationship with Nate. And the surprise wasn't because of him being a stickler for unexpected gifts or uttering super-sweet nothings out of the blue. Confident as Nova was in herself, Nate had always seemed an unlikely match for her. He was popular, massively competitive, and loved having people hanging off his every word, smile or salutation. Nova's natural inclination was to forge her own path, and that had meant she'd actively tried to avoid his charms. And he definitely had a lot of them . . .

But her attitude towards him had seemed to

intrigue Nate, and before she knew it, he'd fully turned his attentions to winning her over. It didn't exactly require too much persuasion – the boy had banter for days and a grin that made her melt, in spite of Nova's attempts to ignore him. He'd finally asked her out six months ago, and as their relationship grew, she had ended up well and truly smitten. On that first date, he'd taken her to a super-fancy Japanese restaurant and winked as he laid one large hand over the prices on the menu. '*Ignore those. Get anything you like, beautiful . . .*'

He'd taken the time to read one of her favourite books just so they could talk about it afterwards. For his sixteenth birthday party, Nate had booked out the whole of the restaurant Nova's family ran, even though she knew that his high-flying parents must have baulked at the idea of a party in the little West African-Caribbean fusion restaurant in the heart of Brixton. And he'd do little things, like avoid holding her hand in the cinema and instead only entwine their little fingers, because he knew Nova found it distracting otherwise. He bought her herb plants instead of flowers because 'they were more useful'. He kissed like an absolute *dream* . . .

That dream had turned into a nightmare when Nova had caught sight of a message flashing up on Nate's phone a couple of months ago. They had been in their favourite dessert place for some supposed study-leave cramming, but mainly sharing way too many slices of cake. Nova had felt blissfully happy, not just from the sugar rush but from being with a guy she'd thought might actually be The One. And then when Nate got up to go to the loo, his mobile phone screen had illuminated with the words that would lead her to heartbreak.

Yeh, obviously. Promise nobody will find out. Tho I can't lie, I'm waiting for you to come to your senses & dump her for me ;)

The name above the message? Amanda Curtis. A girl who had made no secret of her dislike for Nova. As Nate had made his way back to the table, smiling at Nova, he'd seen the expression on her face, then followed her gaze down to his phone and its bombshell display.

'I wasn't looking at it,' Nova had said softly. 'It was just hard to miss.'

Nate had swiped the phone off the table quickly, but the guilt all over his face was impossible to mask. Nova had barely been able to stand his half-hearted excuses, and then he'd taken one deep breath and said, 'To be honest, I've been thinking for a while that this hasn't really been working out . . . and then when we were all round at Finn's the other night . . .'

She'd tuned out as he'd haltingly detailed his encounter with Amanda. Even as he spoke, the irony was that Nova had felt guilty herself. Guilty for thinking, even for a moment, that if she hadn't had the kind of background that required her to work an emergency shift at the family restaurant, she would have been in Finn's fancy conservatory that night too, hanging out with their classmates. Then Nate never would have had the *chance* to end up canoodling with Amanda blinking Curtis. Would he?

Nova had stormed out of the café, trying to hide her tears. But there had been no hiding them only a measly week and a half later, when Nate had decided that lunchtime in the packed school canteen was the perfect time to debut his brand-new relationship with the very girl he'd cheated on Nova with.

She felt sick just *thinking* about the level of humiliation she'd experienced . . .

Gemma caught Nova's eye now, and then sliced hers towards Nate, invisible daggers flying. 'Yeah, we'll come with, as long as you lot are heading there, like, right now?' she said to Tiegen pointedly. 'Otherwise we could catch you at the party later . . .'

'Thank you,' Nova mouthed to Gem while the girls had a quick discussion.

'No worries, hon,' Gemma whispered, then paused and fluffed up her hair in a manner Nova could tell was meant to be nonchalant. 'Unless, of

 13

course, you would rather just head back to yours? You know, maybe we could grab some food and hang out. Um, by the way, is Otis back from that trip to Bristol . . . ?'

She knew why her friend was asking. 'Nah, let's go to the park for a bit,' Nova said with a grin. Even if Gem hadn't ever come out and said it, Nova thought it was plainly obvious that she fancied her older brother something chronic. The girl had practically memorised Otis' college timetable so that she could always be around at the opportune moment to sashay about in front of him!

To Nova's relief some of the girls from their group decided to head to the park, leaving Nate and Clive behind.

'That idiot is fully not worth worrying about anyway,' Gemma reiterated for the hundredth time, linking arms with Nova, who nodded half-heartedly. She knew it was true, but the whole thing still hurt. She was glad when they caught up with the others and talk turned to summer plans as they queued up at the ice-cream van idling at the entrance to the park.

'My mum got me an internship at the paper,' Tiegen was saying, 'which is cool, but I'm sure it'll be mainly making journos cups of tea and that.' She was playing it down massively, Nova knew – Tiegen's mother was the deputy editor of a massive national newspaper, after all.

'How about you, Gem?' one of the others, Ruth, asked, sucking on a disturbingly bright-blue ice lolly.

Nova busied herself telling the man in the ice-cream van her order as Gemma replied.

'Well, bits and bobs really. At least I get two holidays, what with going to Hong Kong with Mum and Mexico with Dad. I'm just hoping his new gold-digger girlfriend isn't going to be there, too . . .' She muttered the last part under her breath, and Nova glanced at her friend. She knew Gemma was having some weirdness with her dad starting to date again. He'd cheated on Gem's mum, which had caused the divorce, and Nova's friend definitely did not approve of this new woman in his life. Still, Gemma sounded more genuinely upbeat as she clapped her hands on Nova's shoulders, making her Flake wobble dangerously. 'And obviously I'll be hanging out with this one! We're heading to Island Rocks Festival next week. It's going to be ah-mazing!'

'Jealous!' Ruth replied. 'Actually, didn't you say you're heading to a few festivals this summer with your family, Nov?'

Nova flipped her locs out of the way, and pulled the chocolate bar eagerly from her ice cream, before biting into it. 'Yeah,' she replied, then chuckled as the delicate curls of chocolate crumbled away down her front. 'My parents run a food truck, so we travel all around the country over the summer usually.'

'Sick!' Tiegen said as they all flopped down under the shade of an oak tree.

Nova shrugged. 'Yeah, it's pretty cool, but I've got to work most of the time.' She knew the other girls rarely had to work unless it was at a

CV-enhancing internship like Tiegen's, but she did her best not to begrudge their privilege. Even Gemma was the daughter of a wealthy Ghanaian businessman and his architect wife – well, ex-wife. Still, Nova loved her family's place, despite the restaurant business being less than glamorous and often quite tough. Her parents had kept their establishment afloat through thick and thin. But while the culinary arts were her mum's true passion, Nova had seen the disappointment in her dad sometimes. Deep down, he'd wanted to make it as a musician, but it hadn't worked out. Maybe that was part of why Nova was so shy of her own musical ambitions.

As she finished off her ice cream, Nova was certain of one more plan for her summer and for the rest of the year, and beyond! She was not planning to be humiliated by Nathan – or any boy – ever again.

And speak of the devil, she could see him and Clive heading towards their group now, and someone else was with them. Nate was clutching

Amanda's hand, and even at this distance, Nova could see the smug smile on her face. As they approached, Amanda leaned up to plant a sloppy kiss on Nate's lips, making him stumble a bit awkwardly.

'Ugh, subtlety personified,' Gemma muttered, scrunching up the plastic wrapper of her ice pop after she sucked up the last of its contents. 'Right, ladies,' she announced, 'me and Nov are going to duck out, I reckon.'

'Fair enough,' Tiegen muttered, shaking her head sympathetically. 'See you later, yeah?'

Nova stood up, trying to give off a positive, unbothered air as Nate and the others got closer. 'Yeah, see you later, guys,' she said, picking up her bag. She avoided Nate's eye as they passed one another, though he had the decency to look a bit sheepish. Gem kissed her teeth, and Nova couldn't help a smile at her friend's open hostility towards her ex-boyfriend. She knew Gemma would do anything for her, and she was massively grateful to have a best mate like her.

'D'you know what?' Gemma asked suddenly, as though a light bulb had gone off in her mind. 'Maybe we need to find you a little summer fling at one of these festivals!'

Nova shook her head, her dreadlocks whipping her cheeks with emphasis as they headed towards the bus stop. 'Nope. No way. I'm done with boys this summer, Gem. I'm just looking forward to getting the heck out of London for a bit. Everywhere I look, there *they* seem to be,' she said, ignoring Gemma's exasperated sigh.

Nova didn't add that she kind of wanted to use the summer free of studying and Nate to compose her own songs, even if she *was* reluctant about sharing them with anyone just yet. Maybe if she found time to write a few more, she'd get the confidence to perform them one day. 'I might even give Sasha's party a miss,' she added.

'Whoa whoa whoa, hon,' Gemma replied, holding up a jazzily manicured hand in Nova's face. 'No man is going to throw a spanner in the works of your social life, OK? Listen, I'll see you later. We don't want to get there too early anyway. I'm coming to yours at eight-thirty with a selection of ensembles and we'll get ready together.'

Nova laughed, knowing there was absolutely no sense in arguing. 'OK, fine. But please try not to bring your whole wardrobe, G?'

'Zero promises,' Gemma replied with a grin, just as Nova's bus pulled up to the stop. 'Laters!'

CHAPTER 2

Nova almost missed her stop as she rapidly scribbled lyrics in her battered purple notebook, headphones playing back the piano chords she'd recorded on her phone the previous night. As she saw the dome of the Brixton Academy loom into view, though, she quickly pressed the bell. The bus ground to a halt, and she rushed down the stairs and out into the familiar streets near her flat. The Academy always filled Nova with a sense of happiness – the music venue had been the scene of many incredible and inspiring musical experiences for her, and she secretly dreamt that maybe one day she might end up on that stage herself.

There go those dreams again . . . she thought; that was the whole idea for the song she'd been crafting on her way home, after all.

As she turned on to her road, the familiar smell of her family's restaurant floated towards her, making her mouth water. It was almost a miracle that it remained one of the most popular eateries in Brixton. Nova knew the area was changing, and long-established places were being edged out by higher rental rates and chain-restaurants that altered the whole feel of the local scene. Still, as Nova approached, she was pleased to see their place was doing a roaring trade this evening.

A couple of the regulars waved through the glass window below the jaunty sign for Eats & Beats, with its Sierra Leonean and Jamaican flags, as Nova passed and pushed the door open. Brass bells jingled above her head as she did, and her eyes swept over the familiar Afrocentric paintings hanging on the walls, and the small cluster of tables covered with brightly coloured cloths adorned with Adinkra symbols or black, green and gold stripes.

The flat Nova lived in with her parents and Otis was above the restaurant, so it was hard to sneak in undetected. She saw that her dad, Hector, was busy in a corner fiddling with one of the speakers, and remembered that it was his open mic night that evening. He held it every couple of weeks, so she knew he would be distracted for a bit setting up. Her mother's voice was coming from the kitchen. Deana was shouting instructions to Otis, who was carrying out plates laden with jollof rice and jerk chicken to a corner table. Nova and her brother often took it in turns to do shifts waiting the tables at the restaurant. Through the hatch that opened up into the kitchen, Nova could see her mum vigorously stirring at the stove with her back turned.

'Did you take that side dish of plantain?' she called without turning around, then continued, 'Or is it still just sitting here going cold?' – clearly knowing full well that Otis would have forgotten it.

Nova chuckled quietly to herself as she tried to sidle in between the tables, heading towards the door at the back of the restaurant that led upstairs to their flat.

'I've only got two ha—' Otis began in a mutter, then in a loud, smug voice proclaimed, 'Ah, *sis*! Just in time!'

Nova scowled at him, and her brother gave her a broad grin in return, then set down the plates at their destined table. 'One sec, yeah, Uncle? *Nova's* just going to grab your plantain.'

The older man at the table smiled up at Otis, dentures sparkling against his dark skin, as he accepted the respectful familiar moniker given to all their elders, whether related or not.

'Yeah, cheers, bruv,' she murmured at him, not because she had an issue with grabbing the side dish and bringing it over, but more because she knew that his announcement meant that—

'Ah ha, my lovely daughter!' her mum said,

wiping her hands on her apron as she stuck her head through the hatch.

Rumbled!

Deana's hair was tied up in her favourite bright green and blue headscarf to prevent some of the smell of the cooking getting into it. 'I can see on your face that you're looking to help out your poor mother.'

Nova handed over the plate Otis had requested, and then leant through the hatch to give her mum a peck on the cheek. 'Um, I was kind of hoping to chill for a bit before this party tonight . . .'

Her mother's face softened. 'I know you've been working hard.' She drew a breath, and Nova knew what was coming next. 'But before you *chill*, I beg, run over the road for your mum, yeah?' Deana chuckled. 'Just a couple of bits . . . A bag of scotch bonnets . . . A tin of callaloo? Make it two. Oh, and another jar of palm oil. And some okra. Actually, maybe I should write it down for you . . .'

'Unlucky,' Otis bent his lanky frame to whisper

to her as he passed, with a grin that suggested he was anything but sympathetic.

Nova resisted the urge to smack him on the back of his freshly shaved fade, and sighed as her mum quickly scribbled down a shopping list on her order notepad, and ripped it off. So much for a bit of telly-watching before Gemma arrived to begin the Project Runway party prep! Still, Nova didn't mind helping – well, not too much.

'Oh, how was your last exam, sweetheart?' her dad asked as he clambered down from the stool he'd been standing on to fix the speaker, his thick dreadlocks swinging down his back.

'Yeah, it was good,' Nova replied. The look on her dad's face was a familiar mixture of pride and determination that his daughter always achieve her absolute best. Nova's mum had gone to culinary college, but her dad had never got further than a few exams back in Jamaica before leaving school. To Nova, they were proof that a fancy degree wasn't necessary to achieve great things, but she knew neither of her parents would swallow that – not if uni could be on the cards for her.

Hector walked over to slip his arm around Deana's waist and plant a kiss emphatically on her temple, and Nova scrunched up her face jokingly at the PDA. She waited for her mum to fish a ten-pound note out of her pocket to run the 'errand' that sounded more like a full-on supermarket sweep. She did like that her parents were still so much in love, though.

The story, as Nova had been told hundreds of times, was that her mum had just got the keys to the restaurant premises when Nova's dad, twenty-five years old and fresh from Jamaica, clutching his guitar, had appeared in the doorway. He'd been booked last-minute with his band to play a support slot at Brixton Academy, and according to the legend, had been drawn towards the delicious food he smelled. Even though it was Sierra Leonean cuisine that Nova's mum was cooking, Hector had apparently decided that it smelled like home the minute he looked at Deana.

 27

His music career had subsequently waned, but as Nova's parents got married and Hector added his own recipes into the mix, their fusion restaurant was born.

Nova smiled to herself thinking of the familiar tale as she turned on her heels to head out to the shops. The sooner she was done, the more time she might have to enjoy actually not having to study, before the party that night.

'I want my change!' her mum called after her, and Nova pursed her lips, but took the opportunity to put her earphones back in and listen to her favourite playlist of contemporary and classic jazz singers.

By the time she got back to the restaurant, the tables had been pushed back slightly from one corner so that the microphones, amplifiers and performance space could be set up. Nova made her way through to the kitchen to drop off the shopping, and a massive grin spread across her face as she saw who was in there alongside her mum.

'Hi, Grandma!' she said, walking over to give her Grandma Rosalind's ample frame a squeeze.

'My shining star! Ah, see how good my granddaughter is, shopping for her mother?' she said with a grin. Nova ignored her mother's raised eyebrow with a small smirk. 'Come, I was just showing your mother how to really season this pepper chicken . . .'

'Been doing it for years, Mum,' Nova's mother mumbled, but Grandma Rosalind was already shaking ingredients into the mixing bowl, ignoring her. Deana rolled her eyes, and Nova laughed. Shoe on the other foot!

'See you in a bit!' she said. 'Oh, when Gem gets here, can you send her up?'

Her mum smiled, even as she said, 'Oh ho, I'm your butler now?'

Nova laughed, grabbing a slice of her dad's ginger cake on her way upstairs to the blessed relief of the flat. Heading into her room, she flopped on to her bed and pulled out her notebook, then slid her mini-keyboard on to the duvet and began picking out the chords she'd been working on. She glanced at her notes, and the lyrics and melody began to come together. Hitting record on her phone, she started to sketch out a song . . .

'Noooo-vaaaa!'

She jumped at the sound of Gemma's voice drifting into the flat. How had two hours passed? She'd been so engrossed in her song-writing that she hadn't even noticed the time. Nova quickly stopped her recording – which had made the phone's memory dangerously close to full anyway – and slid her keyboard down to the floor beside her bed as Gem appeared in the doorway. Her friend's head was barely visible above the massive pile of dresses and clothes in plastic dry-cleaning sacks that she was carrying.

'Good grief, G,' Nova said with a chuckle.

Gemma unloaded her stash of outfits on to the

foot of Nova's bed with an 'ooph'. 'We need options, hon.'

'All that plastic's bad for the environment, you know,' Nova said, but Gemma rolled her eyes.

'I need to keep this stuff pristine. Besides, I'm reusing it. That's environmentally friendly, no?'

Nova was picking up a skirt that seemed more akin to a belt. She looked over at Gemma with a dubious expression.

'Impulse buy,' Gemma said over her shoulder as she began fixing her make-up in the mirror hanging on Nova's wall. Spontaneous shopping was her friend's modus operandi! But Nova had to admit, there were some really cute looks here.

After an hour of trying and rejecting outfits, they were both finally dressed and ready to head to Sasha's party. Nova slung her locs over one shoulder, checking herself out in the mirror – the coral jumpsuit she'd borrowed made her smooth brown skin really shine, she had to admit.

'Gorgeous!' Gemma said before nestling her face next to Nova's for a blinding sequence of selfies. 'I'll send you these,' she said, then quickly grabbed the little handbag which matched her red mini-dress. 'You look *buff*, Nov. Revenge is sweet. Like, Nate who?'

Nova tried to soak in her friend's enthusiasm. She did feel good. Maybe her endless promises to herself that she was finally going to start getting over Nathan were working! She strutted out of the bedroom and down the hallway, twirling dramatically.

'Yess! Serve!' Gemma said, laughing.

They were giggling their way down the stairs, but quietened as they reached the restaurant, noticing that Hector had dimmed the lights and the people eating their meals had hushed a little. Nova and Gemma edged towards the back to watch for a moment. Her dad had already picked up his guitar, alongside Tyrell, his best friend, on bass guitar. Their other bandmate, Michael, was playing a small drum kit. Hector began picking out a soothing, familiar melody, an old tune by the singer Gregory Isaacs. Nova loved his songs –

she couldn't have grown up with Hector Clarke for a dad without getting a real appreciation for reggae music, too! As her father began to sing, she got swept up in the music and almost forgot she and Gemma were on their way out – especially when her dad reached the second chorus. The audience started to clap along, and Hector caught sight of Nova, calling out over the microphone and pointing in her direction.

'I think it's only right my daughter, Nova, join us on this one. What you say, Nova? Come sing with your father!'

She felt her mouth go a bit dry at the thought, even as her mum and Grandma Rosalind came out of the kitchen to watch eagerly. She loved singing with her dad around the flat and stuff, but she always felt an initial shyness when he suggested she take part in the open mic nights.

'Go on, hon,' Gemma said, nudging her with her elbow. 'We're going for "fashionably late" anyway. And you don't fool me, I heard you singing when I came up to the flat earlier!'

Eventually Nova made her way towards the second microphone set up in the performance space as her dad's band stretched out the song's bridge to make time for her to get there. Singing covers, she could just about manage to do in front of people – her own songs, though? Forget about it! Her dad started up on the chorus again, and she cleared her throat. Her voice came through alongside his, and Hector turned to give her a massive grin. She barely noticed as he backed away from his own mic and she began to riff, her vocals soaring as her eyes squeezed closed.

The song finished and she opened them to a rousing round of applause. Nova felt a tiny bit of embarrassment as she hustled away from the spotlight, mumbling thanks as people congratulated her.

'My daughter, Nova Clarke!' her dad announced again with a flourish, as though they were at a full-on concert not just their restaurant's open mic night.

'Ah-mazing!' Gemma exclaimed as Nova

reached her side again.

At least any encounter with Nate at the party wouldn't be more embarrassing than going full Mariah in front of a whole roomful of people without even thinking about it!

'Let's get out of here!'

CHAPTER 3

A week later, Nova was grabbing clothes out of her wardrobe to fold into her huge backpack, ready for her departure to Island Rocks the next morning. Mixed feelings overwhelmed her as she pushed aside the jumpsuit she'd worn to Sasha's party, which in her classic way, Gem had insisted Nova should keep. *'As if I could compete with how good you looked in that thing, babe!'* While it was really generous of her, Nova knew that her best mate had also been trying to soothe the burn of having seen Nate and Amanda making a real display of themselves at Sasha's soirée.

Nova had tried to ignore it, but it hadn't worked. As Nate and his new girlfriend flaunted their relationship in front of her, she'd fled to the bathroom for a crying session. Gem, Tiegen and Ruth had kept up a stream of loo roll, shouting at the people banging on the door to wait their turn.

'Ugh,' Nova muttered now, as the radio show she was streaming decided to taunt her with a song that *she* and Nate had danced to not long after they'd made their relationship official. Launching herself at her computer, she switched off the show and put on some nice, safe Billie Holliday. She sighed with relief as the singer's mournful, beautiful voice filled the air. At least Lady Day understood her pain!

It was still embarrassing to think that she wasn't over the whole Nate thing yet, but at least she was getting away tomorrow. The Island Rocks festival was going to be a welcome escape, even if most of the time Nova would be helping out on the food truck. When she was younger, travelling to festivals with her parents and Otis was the highlight of her summer. It was so exciting – the sights and sounds, the food of course, but most of all, the music. Summertime was always a bit quiet for the restaurant, so when Nova was ten, her mum and dad had decided to invest in the truck and combine Hector's love of music with Deana's entrepreneurial culinary spirit and take Eats & Beats on the road. The thing was, the older Nova got, the more she wished she could have a bit more time to explore the festivals on her own. Especially now that her mates were going to be living their best lives swaying in the crowds, while Nova was stuck serving food to worse-for-wear festivalgoers.

Still, she didn't plan on complaining. Packing complete, Nova decided to take some inspiration from Billie and work on a new song, about the feelings Nathan Kahale-Turner had brought up. Grabbing her phone and hitting record, she free-styled a composition with a bluesy edge about thinking you know someone, but not really knowing him – ahem, *them* – at all. All the best songs were about love, but this time Nova planned to exorcise the love she'd felt for Nate.

'Land ahoy!'

Nova chuckled as her mum gripped the railing of the ferry's upper deck excitedly and pointed towards the horizon. The Isle of Wight was slowly coming into view, with summer sunshine glistening off the water.

'Don't mind me, eh?' her mum added, as Nova returned to scanning the online festival program on her phone. She was trying to compile a list of the most important acts she wanted to check out while she was there, but it was proving pretty challenging. She sighed, realising the Ivorian drum virtuoso she had been planning to catch was scheduled on a different stage at exactly the same time as ¡Mami!, a Spanish rapper who Nova had seen interviewed while cruising YouTube last week.

Choices, choices . . .

'Don't forget you'll need to fit all that in around your shifts on the truck,' her mum pointed out to her, zipping her brightly coloured lightweight cagoule a little higher.

'How could I?' Nova mumbled. Even with the annoying reminders of work, she'd enjoyed having a bit of time to spend with her mum solo while they made their way to the festival – her dad and Otis had decided to drive the truck over to the site a day earlier with Hector's bandmates in tow. They had a little show on one of the smaller stages, and Nova knew her dad was really excited to be playing at Island Rocks, even if it was a short set.

'I know you'll want to clear the decks to see Flightpath headlining, though,' Deana teased, mirth dancing in her brown eyes before she slipped her sunglasses on to shield them from the glare.

'Har har,' Nova retorted. She had never really understood the appeal of that band. Their music was inoffensive enough, but the phrase 'middle of the road' could have been invented for them. Despite that, she was pretty sure she'd heard her dad playing a reggae version of their biggest hit 'Be the Change', but then she could say the same about numerous Celine Dion songs. Everything sounded better with an island lilt.

Nova finally looked up from the app on her phone as her mum put her arm around her shoulders, looking at her sincerely. 'Don't worry, sweetheart, I'll make sure you have some breaks to go and check out your favourite bands. I want you to have a bit of time to enjoy yourself this summer before A levels start, eh?'

There were those academic hopes again. But for now, Nova absolutely planned to enjoy herself. She glanced back down at her screen as a message came through, and grinned as she saw Gemma's name.

OMW hon! The glamping site better have an emphasis on *glam*!! Sooo excited, will let you know the minute I get there. Have some Eats n Beats grub ready!

This was followed by her usual avalanche of emojis, and a gif for good measure. Nova definitely planned to do everything she could to make sure Island Rocks lived up to its name!

By the time she and her mum had disembarked from the ferry, Nova's stomach was rumbling, and she was hoping that Otis and her dad would have arrived and got some nosh going. They made their way to the buses that were conveying festival-goers from the docks to the site, and Nova felt a thrill of excitement as she saw the location come into view. Massive stages were dotted across the fields, which were thankfully looking relatively dry and grassy. No rain had been forecast – for now at least – which was good news. She hiked her backpack on to her shoulders and she and her mum followed the signs towards the camping area for caterers, near to where the food trucks would be set up. Nova broke into a trot as she spotted the Eats & Beats truck with its bright decals parked up. Her dad and Otis were working away to set up the awning outside it. She was also kind of hoping they'd already set up the tents, so that she didn't have to struggle with poles and mattress pumps.

'Hey!' Hector called, ambling over to greet them, kissing her mum on the lips and squeezing Nova tightly in a hug. 'Made it!'

Otis squinted over at them in the bright sunlight, and Deana went over to give him a hug.

'Hey, sis,' he said, giving her his customary fist bump. 'Just in time for tents!'

Nova screwed up her face. 'Yeah, nice one. Bet you saved that just for me.' She grabbed a couple of cold patties from the Tupperware her dad had packed snacks in, and then she and her brother made their way through the back of the food area to the campsite. They got the tents up in relatively quick time – one for her, one for him and one for their parents.

'Pump! Pump! Pump!' she instructed through her laughter as Otis sweated, working the foot pump to inflate the mattresses. He'd lost a coin toss fair and square, but soon they were ready to

 43

head back and start helping out at the truck.

'Hey, you two!' called a red-headed, velvet-clad lady with a big grin as they passed through the campsite. 'Great to see you!'

'Wendy, hi!' Nova went over to give the woman a hug, and inhaled the delicious scent of doughnuts that was clinging to her. Wendy made the best sugary sourdough creations Nova had ever tasted! They knew a lot of the other people running catering and food trucks from having worked the festival circuit for so many years. 'We'll be over for dessert in a bit!'

'Do! I've even made a doughnut inspired by a recipe Hector gave me – rum and banana.'

Otis clutched his stomach. Clearly the patty Nova had pilfered for him had barely touched the sides. 'Mmmmm,' he groaned. 'We'll be there ASAP!'

They went over to find that their parents had already connected the truck to the gas and electricity, and were getting started on food prep. It was only three o'clock in the afternoon, and the festival wasn't fully underway yet, but Nova knew that the early arrivals and the other catering and backstage staff would be keen to start getting hold of some grub by early evening. Sighing, she washed her hands, tied on her apron and got to work alongside her family in the cramped space of the food truck. Her dad cranked up his latest mix of reggae and afrobeats, and Nova had to admit it was a fun affair. She sang some harmonies over the music, safe with just her family around, and decided this was going to be one of the best summers ever. She hadn't even thought about Nate and his shenanigans once since—

Oh. Almost. She would have to do better. *Boy-free summer!* she reminded herself.

CHAPTER 4

'One, twooooo . . . One, twooo. Check-uh. Check-uh, one, twooo . . . one, twooo . . .'

'Gaaah!' Nova uttered, attempting to stuff her head under her pillow on the inflated mattress in her tent. But it was no use – it was only eight in the morning, but already things were well and truly getting underway at the Island Rocks site. Some roadie was doing the loudest mic check in history on a stage nearby, with absolutely no consideration for Nova's beauty sleep.

As she gave up and unzipped her tent, she was greeted with warm sunshine that lifted her spirits a bit. They were sapped again, though, when she made her way to the communal showers and toilets and saw the state they were in. Swimming costume on, shower shoes on, XL shower cap to cover her locks, and a very rapid scrubbing technique *just about* got her through it. Her expression was still set to 'traumatised' as she made her way back to her tent, and Otis, who was just emerging from his own tent, laughed grimly.

'That great, eh?'

'I don't get how they're already so rank,' Nova said, shaking her head. No matter how many festival loos and showers she encountered, they were the one part of the experience that she could more than do without. As she finished throwing on her clothes in her tent – fresh shorts, a customised blue-and-yellow striped sleeveless top, and her favourite wide-brimmed hat and Doc Marten boots – she heard her phone ringing.

'Up you get, Nov,' her mum said cheerily down the line.

'I *am* up!' Nova protested, but her mum continued.

'Well, we're already at the truck! Your dad decided to get some ackee and saltfish going for the breakfast punters, and I'm trying to make some banana fritters. Grab your brother and come give us a hand, the line's getting kind of hefty . . . !'

Nova didn't bother suppressing another grimace as she watched her brother swipe at his armpits with some biodegradable baby wipes, then pull on his T-shirt and declare himself good to go. At least he washed his hands thoroughly once they got to the food truck. Then they put on the old faithful disposable gloves (Nova had spent ages scouring the internet trying to find compostable ones) and got to work helping their parents with the customers eagerly ordering their breakfast. By mid-morning, Nova was starting to flag, but then a voice in front of the truck cut through the gathering noise of the early acts on the stages nearby.

'I. Have. ARRIVED!'

Nova squealed, then broke into a huge grin as she saw Gemma elbowing hungry festival-goers out of the way to get to the front of the queue. 'Yes, babe!' she shouted through the hatch, abandoning her bowl of mashed bananas to make her way out of the truck and give Gemma a massive hug. She pulled back, chuckling as she took in her friend's attire. Impossibly short denim cut-offs clung to her curvy frame, barely visible under some kind of sequined poncho, and she wore bright purple (and totally unnecessary) Hunter wellies on her feet that Nova knew would have cost a fortune. Completing the look were white-framed oversized sunglasses, with her weave twisted into a bun atop her head.

'You look wicked!' Nova told her friend, as Gemma waved enthusiastically towards Deana and Hector, reserving a special wink for Otis.

'Well, you know, I thought I'd make an effort,' Gemma said, still peering over Nova's shoulder towards her brother. Eventually she returned her gaze to her friend, looking Nova up and down.

'Which is more than I can say for this ensemble, babe. I mean . . . Wow. Functional, sure. But, like, where's the pizzazz? We need to harness the energy of this festival, really get our sparkle going, know what I mean? Ooh, are those fritters . . . ?' She wandered over to the hatch from which Otis was serving breakfast to a pair of giggling Spanish girls. Ignoring their dirty looks, Gemma smiled up at Nova's brother, adjusting her poncho and looking over the frames of her sunglasses. 'Hey, O.'

Nova rolled her eyes at Gemma's breathy voice.

'All right, Gem? How's it going?' Otis replied, taking in Gemma's attention-grabbing outfit. The girls he'd been flirting with retreated, muttering to one another.

'Nov?' her mum called from inside the truck, then emerged from the truck wiping her brow. She paused to give Gemma a peck on the cheek in greeting. 'Looking very spangly, Gemma love! Fantastic!'

'Thanks! Matter of fact, I was just saying our girl here could do with a little sprucing up herself, get her into the spirit of things. Would it be OK to steal her away for a bit?'

Deana nodded, chuckling as she smoothed her hands down her apron. 'I was just going to say, Nov, you can grab a break now. We'll get started on the lunch prep. Long as you're back here by half twelve, yeah?'

Nova wasn't sure if she wanted to be unleashed into the hands of Gemma for a sartorial makeover, but a couple of hours off sounded good. 'Cool, will do. Thanks, Mum!'

She linked arms with her friend, but then tried to put the brakes on her wellied stride when she saw she was being steered towards a tent ominously called 'The Glitter Experience'.

'Nah, no way, Gem. Glitter is bad for the environment, for a start, and—'

Gemma clamped Nova's arm tighter and dragged her towards the entrance. 'Relax, hon! It's the boutique where I picked up this bad boy,' she said, fluffing out her sparkly top. 'We should get you one, too!'

Before Nova knew what was happening, they were inside the tent full of brightly coloured, twinkling racks of clothing, and Gemma was holding up items to her front.

'Ah! This one! Hello? Yes!'

Nova had to admit that the blue halter-neck, trimmed with tiny mirrored sequins, was pretty damn near perfection. But . . . 'This is way too expensive, Gem.'

'Don't be stupid, it's my treat!'

Nova sighed. Sometimes Gemma's generosity made her feel a bit inadequate. Not to mention the fact that her friend always seemed to want to give her dad's credit card a workout. Maybe it was some kind of subconscious revenge on him for breaking their family up?

Gemma clearly saw Nova's expression, and let out a long sigh of her own. 'Look, if you really don't want it . . .'

Nova hated being the cause of the disappointed look on her friend's face. And it *was* a pretty amazing top. 'All right, all right. But that's it for the summer, yeah? I can't keep up with this level of generosity!'

Gemma squealed in delight and headed towards the little cash register set up in one corner. 'Think of it as a super-early birthday pressie.'

'My birthday's not till October.'

'Well, whatever.' Gemma looked over her shoulder at the till, and Nova came to a halt beside her. 'Besides, Nov, you're generous in ways I could never repay. You're always there for me . . .' She drew in a breath as Nova gave her friend's arm a squeeze.

'Of course I am,' Nova said. 'Just know I'm here whenever you want to talk, hon.'

Gem shook her head. 'Look, don't worry. Let's not do all that right now.' She slapped the card down on the counter and gave the cashier a bright smile, then turned to Nova. 'We're getting you into that top!'

Ten minutes later, halter-top on, Nova felt the heat of the sun on her bare back as she and Gemma left the boutique tent. She caught sight of her reflection in a mirror outside one of the other stalls, and almost didn't recognise the face smiling back at her. It had been a while since she'd felt so carefree – no exams, no rules (well, sort of), no *Nate*, just her and her best mate! She chuckled to herself at the unintentional rhyme, but then was startled by a honking horn that made her and Gemma jump out of the way. A golf buggy zoomed past them with little regard for the festival-goers picking their way across the fields. A kaftan-wearing, willowy brunette sat in the back of it, filming the scene on her phone.

'Oh my gosh, babe, do you know who that was?' Gemma said, watching the vehicle speed away from them. Nova shook her head. '*Sadie Varma!*'

Nova looked at her friend blankly, and Gemma pulled off her oversized sunglasses, as if she was aghast at Nova's ignorance. 'Sadie Varma?' she repeated. 'Like, one of the biggest influencers out there right now? And she's going out with that guy . . . Like, all fit and vegan . . . Lead singer of FlightPath?'

'You think *Clay Cooper* is fit?' Nova enquired, pulling a face.

'Well, at least you know who *he* is, then,' Gemma said. 'Besides, yeah, why not? He's got a sort of crinkly, rock star kind of vibe. You know I like older men.' She winked, and Nova pulled even more of a face, before they both started laughing.

'Listen, G, if you heard the volume of Otis' snoring, which I could hear from my tent *next door* this morning, you'd relax on the whole "fancying my brother" thing,' Nova said, still chuckling, but Gemma had already been distracted by one of the other nearby stalls.

'Ooh, I saw an ad online for one of those!' she exclaimed, bustling over to where a tall, sun-bleached blond guy was demonstrating the supposed ease with which he could inflate a bright pink lounge-chair-sofa-thing. Nova looked on sceptically as his face grew redder with each attempt, but Gemma was somehow sold on it immediately. 'Nov, this is perfect. My yurt is nice and that, but not really comfy for just *hanging out*, know what I mean?'

'Why would you need to hang—' But Gemma clearly wasn't listening.

'I'm thinking I could get one of these and make a sort of lounge area so I can hang out and *read* when you're busy with the truck.' She mentioned her favourite pastime rapturously. 'And then I can take it back for our garden for the summer . . .'

When Gemma got *that look* on her face, Nova knew it was very unlikely she'd be able to talk her friend out of it. Gem was already handing over her cash to the red-faced man and told him that she'd take the one he was holding, since it was already inflated.

'That'll save me the effort, eh?' Gemma said to Nova, taking the unwieldy inflated chair off his hands.

'Isn't the whole point that—' But her friend was already heading away with the chair bouncing against her hip, dance-shuffling towards a tent that was emitting a pumping rhythm. Nova had to admit she was finding herself drawn in by the beat, too. She caught up with Gemma and the two of them pushed aside the colourful beads that shrouded the entrance to the tent the music was coming from.

The space was bathed in multi-coloured light coming from numerous bulbs that were hanging up around the interior, casting a strange glow over the people inside. They were all moving their bodies enthusiastically to the DJ's beats. She was a stunning woman with an enormous afro. She clasped one cup of her headphones to her ear, grinning widely as the next tune came in and the crowd went wild. Despite the fact that the chair Gemma was still clutching was forcing people to move out of the way, they cheered her on good-naturedly with pats on the back as she made her way to the centre of the floor. She grabbed Nova's hands and they danced around the inflatable sofa with others joining in. It was that kind of party!

Everyone was skimpily dressed, which seemed just as well because it was unbelievably hot in there. Nova lost track of the time as they danced, until her phone buzzed in the pocket of her shorts. At first she hadn't been sure it wasn't just the pulse of the music, but as she pulled it out, she saw a few messages from her brother.

Where ru?

Sis, the line is mad already.

N, are u having a laugh? Get back here!!

Whoops! She leaned over to shout at Gemma over the music, 'Babe, I've got to get back to the van.' She was pretty gutted to have to leave, but there was no point risking her mum's wrath. Luckily, Gemma didn't seem too sad to be abandoned – a group of three slightly older girls wearing matching fluffy bikinis kept trying to envelop her friend in a dancing circle.

'Ahh, rubbish!' she shouted. 'But fair enough, hon. I think I'm gonna hang out with these lot for a bit, but I'll come and find you later, yeah?' She began to shimmy again, but then thought of something. 'Ooh, ooh, ooh, hang on. Nov? Can you do me a maaaassive favour?'

Nova knew she wouldn't be *maaaassively* keen on whatever came out of Gemma's mouth next.

'Could you take the chair over to the food truck with you, and I'll come and grab it later?'

Her expression was clearly less than enthusiastic, because Gemma's turned into her most pleading, wide-eyed look. 'Go on, pleaaasee? I wouldn't ask, but it's miles to go back to the glamping site, and these girls were saying that they want to head over to the HeartBeat stage in ten or so. DJ Killswitch is playing, and there's no way I'll be able to—'

Holding up her hands in submission, Nova bent down to pick up the chair. 'Fine, fine, I'll take it. But only because you got me this!' she said, shaking her torso to make her top sparkle. She leaned over and pecked Gemma on the cheek. 'See you later, yeah? Be good!'

Her friend nodded, but was already spinning away towards her new mates. Nova didn't begrudge Gem having fun – at least *she* was going to be able to let her hair down at Island Rocks! Nova, on the other hand, had a feeling her obligations at the food truck would occupy a lot of her time. Still, this morning had been fun. She smiled apologetically at dancing punters as she made her way out of the tent, barely able to see over the top of the chair.

As she emerged out through the beaded curtain covering the exit and the pumping music faded behind her, Nova tried to deflate the thing as she walked back towards the food area, dodging people relaxing on the ground or wandering from tents to stages to stalls. She was muttering to herself, struggling with the chair through the crowd, when she suddenly felt herself slam into a tall, sturdy frame.

'Arg!' Nova exclaimed, as she felt something

warm and messy smush into her brand-new top. Looking down, she saw the remains of a paper plate full of chips, all smeared in ketchup and mayonnaise, on the ground around her feet. Lowering the semi-inflated chair, Nova's brow was already furrowed, and she was ready to emit a South London 'oi!' – but as she made eye contact with the guy she'd collided with, the exclamation died on her lips.

Wow! He. Is. FIT.

CHAPTER 5

'Sorry about that,' she mumbled, half-expecting an apology in return, even though *sorry* was not going to sort out the sauce now working its way into the sequins of her beautiful new halter-top! But as she stared up at the boy, who was looking down at her with an amused expression, she again lost her train of thought.

He was tall with broad shoulders, a deep tan, and thick, long-ish, curly, messy dark hair that he pushed back with one hand, using the other to brush down his dark green T-shirt. It almost matched the colour of his eyes as they glinted in the sunlight.

'Yeah, I'm sorry about it, too. I'm *super* hungry,' he said with a chuckle, putting his hands on his hips and squinting at her, making no effort to move out of Nova's way. 'Uh, is that some kind of couch, or . . . ?' He gestured to the inflatable, which was now looking significantly more deflated.

'Long story,' she mumbled, reaching down awkwardly to pick it up.

'You want me to get that for you?' he asked, but Nova shook her head then flicked her locs out of her face. Was she imagining it or did this boy have an American accent?

'Nope, I can manage,' she said, glancing away from the lingering interrogation of the boy's stare. She was having a hard time wrestling the inflatable into a position she could keep walking with, though, and he continued watching her.

'Where you headed to in such a hurry anyway?'

Nova pursed her lips, but then found herself saying, 'I'm late for work, if you must know.'

'Oh, I must,' he said, still with that expression of suppressed amusement. He ambled along beside her as Nova tried and failed to pick up her pace.

'Look, sorry about your chips, but I've got to go.' She was even more sorry about her new top, but to be fair, it wasn't totally his fault. Nova was pretty sure that if *she* had been paying attention, she would have noticed him. He was pretty hard to miss . . .

'No problem,' the guy said. He was still walking along beside her, and with her slow progress, Nova was pretty sure she was due a major ticking off by the time she actually got back to the food truck. 'I wasn't enjoying them anyhow. Like I said, I was just hungry,' he continued with a shrug, tilting his head to one side and smiling at her. 'Looks like you're heading back to where the food's at, too, huh?'

Why was he still following her? Out of the corner of her eye, Nova noticed now that something was bumping across his back, and realised that he was carrying a small acoustic guitar. It was strapped across his middle, pulling his T-shirt taut across his clearly muscular torso.

No, that isn't distracting at all!

'Guess I'm headed back that way, too.' He glanced at her and laughed a little at her struggling along with the chair.

'Sure you don't want me to give you a hand with that?' he asked, and she shook her head again. She was very conscious that she must be looking a bit of a state, with condiments smeared all down her front, but she tried not to think about it. Why should it even matter? She had no idea who this bloke was! *No boys, remember?*

'Uh, yeah, I'm sure,' she said sarcastically. But as she spoke, Nova stumbled again, almost tripping over the legs of a girl wearing fuzzy pink boots as she sprawled out on the grass with a blissed-out expression on her face.

'Woah, there!' the boy said to Nova, reaching out to steady her with one strong arm. 'You know what, since we're headed in the same direction, I'm gonna have to insist on carrying that thing.' He reached for the inflatable before Nova could protest, scooping it up easily. 'So, do you always carry your own seating?' he asked with a teasing grin.

She shot a frown in his direction. 'It's my mate's actually, I'm just doing her a favour.'

He held his free hand up in protest, still smiling at her. Nova felt herself begin to sweat. She told herself it was just from the warm weather. 'All right. Well, you're a good friend, because this thing is *ugly*,' he said.

'Thanks for your opinion,' she said, then pursed her lips, even though obviously she agreed. They were getting closer to the food trucks, and Nova wasn't quite sure how she was going to ditch him. Or even if she wanted to . . .

'So, you were telling me about your work?'

'I don't think I was, actually,' she replied, trying to ignore his seemingly unshakeable mischievous grin. 'I'm just helping out my family on their food truck,' she added grudgingly.

His eyes – such a distractingly sparkling emerald – lit up at that. 'Oh, word? Hook me up! Come on, it's the least you could do.'

Nova couldn't help a half-surprised, half-amused chuckle at his audacity. 'What makes you think that?'

'Well, my plate of food all over the ground back there, for one.'

Wordlessly, Nova reached over to take the chair back, but he pulled it away. 'OK, fine. My bad, Chair Chick. It was *both* our faults,' he said, with that grin again. *Chair Chick? Who is this guy?* 'I'm gonna come hit up your truck though, replace my lunch.'

'You don't even know what kind of food it is. Maybe you'll hate it,' she said. 'A plate of chips doesn't exactly scream "adventurous diner".'

He shrugged. 'First thing I came across. Usually I'd grab something at the catering tent, but the offering today was pretty busted. Some kind of nasty pasta.'

Was he working here too or something? Nova tried not to let her curiosity get the better of her.

'So what kinda food is it, then?' he asked.

'Hmm? Oh. Um, it's a fusion. Caribbean and

West African.' She raised an eyebrow towards him, gauging his reaction.

'Dope! My mom's from the Caribbean. Well, Cuba.'

Nova assessed him again. 'Oh, right. Uh, this is Jamaican food. My dad's side. And Sierra Leonean from my mum's.'

'I'm uh . . . I'm Sam, by the way.' He seemed to pause, and then looked her in the eye. 'Sam Rodriguez.' He held his hand out to her as she walked beside him, and Nova glanced at it before meeting his eye again and shaking it.

'Nova Clarke,' she said, 'if we're being formal.' He held on to her hand a second longer than seemed strictly necessary.

'Anyway – you were telling me about your folks?'

Nova raised an eyebrow again. 'Was I?' He laughed, and she tried to ignore the musical sound of it. 'Are you playing here or something?' she asked, nodding to his guitar.

Sam shrugged. 'Hope so, maybe, if I track down

an open mic. And besides, I don't like to leave *mi preciosa* lonely,' he said, touching the guitar's strap for a moment.

Is this guy serious? Still, she was intrigued in spite of herself. 'Are you working here, then? Or do you just like to sneak your way into the catering tents?'

He seemed to hesitate for a moment, and Nova almost regretted striking up more conversation with him, but then Sam said, 'Not exactly. My . . . My dad's working here. I'm staying with him for the summer. I guess I kind of grew up around festivals and shows.' He looked down at the ground.

Ah, his dad's probably a roadie, Nova thought, nodding. They had reached the food trucks, and were only a few metres away from Eats & Beats now.

'Yeah, same,' she said, slowing down to a stop. 'We've done the circuit every summer for ages now.' She cocked her head to one side. 'But your accent sounds like you should be at Palm Springs

Village Fest rather than Island Rocks?'

He chuckled, and let the inflatable chair come to rest on the grass next to him as if he was in no hurry to get his food now. 'Wot, eye don't sound like ahm from round 'ere?' he said in a painful approximation of an English accent.

'Wow,' Nova said, genuinely laughing now. 'Do *not* do that again.' Her laughter seemed to please Sam, and she held a hand to her mouth to try and stifle it. His gaze remained unrelenting as ever.

He folded his arms and nodded. 'Busted. I am half British, though – my dad.' But then his eyes grew serious. Nova knew she should really be getting to the truck – she'd be in extra trouble if her mum and dad, or worse still Otis, spotted her just standing around chatting – but she was intrigued when Sam continued, 'This is his big drive to reconnect.' He scuffed one battered Converse against the grass, looking down. 'I live in Miami with my mom, but he was pretty insistent I come bond or whatever this summer.' He shook his head, as if clearing it of some train of thought. He looked back up at her. 'Could be worse, huh? And things have definitely taken a turn for the better in the past ten minutes . . .'

He was actually flirting with her! Nova flushed and reached down for the chair, trying to disregard this development. Drawing in a breath, she said, 'Well, I'm due for a hiding if I don't get my behind over there,' she said, nodding in the direction of Eats & Beats.

Sam rubbed his hands together and made an exaggerated lip-smack. 'OK,' he said appraisingly, looking over at the food truck. 'Bring it on!'

Nova rolled her eyes, but still couldn't hide a slight smile as they made their way over. She told Sam to wait off to the side while she went around to the back, dumping Gemma's ridiculous chair behind the truck before climbing the small metal stairs that led inside. The heat of cooking hit her, and she was ready to face the wrath of her mum, but the queue was too busy for Deana to do much more than give Nova a stern look and tap the air above her watch with one disposable-gloved finger.

Otis, on the other hand, had time. 'Good of you to join us, sis!' he said, lifting his apron over his head. 'And, oh look – time for my break!'

He grinned broadly at Nova, handing over the apron and making his way out of the truck, to zero protest from her mum and dad. Hector was stirring a massive pot of curry goat on the little burner, and the smell of the freshly made food began to make Nova's mouth water. Her mum was simultaneously frying plantain and checking on the electric cooker filled with fluffy white rice.

'Nova, darling, pick up on the orders, OK? TWO PEANUT STEW!'

Nova was confused at that last exclamation as her mum was still looking at her, while somehow also managing to spoon rice into two of the environmentally friendly bamboo containers they'd sourced in a job lot online. Deana only looked away to cover the rice with her delicious signature peanut butter stew with chicken, and

 72

then two punters came up to the window of the truck eagerly.

Ah, order ready!

Nova took the containers and handed them over, then held up the card reader for the girl to pay. Her boyfriend was already tucking into the food.

'Omagawd,' Nova heard him say through a mouthful, as they headed away from the truck. 'Delicious!'

She had to take three more people's orders straight away, all the time aware of Sam hovering off to the side, still eagerly waiting for his free grub. Nova could feel his eyes on her, and whenever she glanced over he'd clutch his stomach feigning extreme hunger. Finally she gestured him across, and he pretended to stagger as he made his way to the truck. He leaned his brown forearms on the little ledge in front of the truck's serving window when he reached it, smiling up at Nova.

She melted slightly, but made a point of rolling her eyes at him. 'You could have just gone to one of the other trucks, you know,' she told him.

He shook his head. 'After seeing the rapture on people's faces after eating here? No way.' He turned to take a look at the menu jauntily written on a board off to the side of the serving window. 'Oh, man, where to start? I'll go from the top. One large curry goat with rice, please, ma'am.'

She nodded, and turned to tell her dad the order. He dished it up quickly, and Nova handed it over to Sam. He sniffed it and closed his eyes, giving an exaggerated sigh of pleasure. Nova couldn't help checking him out while he wasn't looking, and blushed as his lids flew open again. 'Nah, for real, this smells really good. I feel bad not paying.' He reached around to pull a wallet out of his back pocket but Nova shook her head.

'Deal's a deal, I suppose.'

Sam smiled widely, returning his wallet to his jeans and picking up one of the sustainably sourced wooden forks from the pot on the ledge, taking a mouthful of curry. 'Wow. This is unbelievable!'

'Glad to hear it.' She felt her shy smile on her lips, but Sam began to eat enthusiastically, and she cleared her throat, nodding to the next person in the line – a bearded giant of a man who started to place his order loudly over Sam's shoulder.

'I guess you've gotta give the people what they want,' Sam said to her. 'Thanks a bunch for this. I'll be back, like Arnie said.'

'Uh-huh,' she replied, taking down the big man's order on a notepad and handing it over to her mum.

'OK, *that* was corny,' Sam said, beginning to stride away. He winked at her, and called back, 'But I meant it, Nova Clarke.'

CHAPTER 6

It was the next afternoon. Nova felt a rush of air gust out of her lungs as she sank back gratefully on the throw Gemma had arranged on the ground near the food truck, amongst all the other festival-goers who were sitting down to enjoy their grub.

'Ugh, my feet are killing me!' she exclaimed up at the sky, then felt the soft fabric under her palms. 'Is this thing cashmere or something?'

'Babe, I'm not crazy, would I picnic on cashmere?' Gemma said, lying next to Nova. 'It's a silk blend thing I think,' she added nonchalantly.

Nova raised her sunglasses to stare at her friend pointedly, but Gemma didn't seem to notice.

'Did Otis make these dumplings?' she asked, sitting up and examining the food Nova had brought over, then glancing eagerly over towards the truck with a wave and a thumbs-up at him.

Nova sighed, replaced her shades and closed her eyes. 'Rude. That is all my handiwork, I'll have you know!' The lunch rush had finally tailed off, and Nova was looking forward to having a bit of time off to soak up the sun and some music.

Early this morning she had awoken after a dream – or should that be *nightmare* – about Nate. They had been at the festival, snuggling up together under the night sky as one of Nova's favourite bands played. But then somehow they'd got separated in the crowd, and she'd found herself growing increasingly panicked, tapping people who looked like Nate from behind on the shoulder, only to find when they turned around they weren't him. At last, she had spotted him among the jostling bodies watching the performance – and he was kissing someone else. She'd woken up breathless and upset. She was fairly sure her dream had something to do with that Sam Rodriguez guy – his confusing flirtation, his handsome face, his tall, strong physique . . .

Ugh, stop it, Nova!

She hadn't bothered mentioning to Gemma her encounter with Sam the day before. There was nothing to tell, right? She wasn't looking for any kind of relationship right now. If that dream had told her anything, it was warning her that she was still processing Nate's betrayal. The last thing Nova felt she needed was another boy who would undoubtedly break her heart in the end. She'd probably never see Sam again anyway. There were thousands of people at the festival. It wasn't like he was . . . *standing over her right now!*

'Hey there,' Sam said. He was casting a shadow over her from head to toe, his acoustic guitar strap criss-crossing the front of his T-shirt again. The tee was white this time, with a sketch of someone who, even upside down, Nova could tell was one of her favourite artists in the world – Amy Winehouse.

'Err, hi,' Nova choked out, sitting up quickly and adjusting her yellow vest-top. She noticed he was eating a large serving of her mum's peanut stew and rice, holding the container casually in one large hand. 'What are you doing here?' *Duh – what does it look like, Nova?*

'Well,' he said, smiling down at her, 'I came across this incredible food truck yesterday, and I've been struggling to get it out of my mind. Though I've gotta say, the server was a lot cuter then . . .'

Before she could respond, Gemma was holding her hand up towards Sam, while staring between him and Nova in a massively unsubtle way, a huge grin on her face. 'And who do we have here?' she asked, as Sam shook her hand good-naturedly. 'I'm Gemma, Best Friend,' she added, like it was her job title.

'Sam,' he replied. 'Uh, new friend, I guess?'

'Sit, Sam,' Gemma said, patting the throw before Nova could protest.

He walked around towards Nova's feet and folded his long legs into an easy crossed position in front of them, setting his food down and sweeping his guitar off his back in one smooth motion. His eyes lingered on her a moment before returning to Gemma. 'Thanks. You must be the friend who likes impractical inflatable furniture.'

'Guilty,' Gemma said with a chuckle.

'Well I'm glad, because if it wasn't for your couch, I wouldn't have met your buddy here,' Sam said. Why were they gabbing like Nova wasn't even there? She cleared her throat, and they both turned towards her.

'I'm less glad,' Nova said to Gem, 'because it's also the reason the brand-new top you got me is currently encrusted with condiments.'

Sam made an apologetic face, then took another mouthful of his food. 'I'm trying to make it up in food truck patronage. Though to be honest it is no chore. This is freakin' delicious.'

'Are you a Yank, Samuel?' Gemma asked, clearly amused by this whole situation.

'Guilty,' he replied, mimicking her. 'Nova didn't fill you in on me?' He clutched one hand to his chest feigning hurt, and Nova felt herself flush. 'Let's see,' he said, 'I am indeed a Yank. Well, Cubano-American. And kind of a Brit, I guess. I'm here for the summer to appease my pops. Nova ruined my lunch yesterday, and then she *begged* me to let her make it up to me. I mean, the grovelling was embarrassing really.'

'Inaccurate,' Nova interjected, though she couldn't help smiling. 'Nice T-shirt,' she added.

'Thanks,' Sam said, looking down at it. 'Amy was the truth,' he said wistfully. He set down his nearly empty container of food and picked up his guitar, strumming a few lines of one of Nova's favourite songs of hers.

'She was,' Nova replied softly, absentmindedly singing along before she felt self-conscious and stopped.

'This one is *constantly* singing her tunes,' said Gemma proudly. 'Sometimes I'm like, has Amy inhabited her body or what? Vocalsssss!'

She nudged Nova, who desperately wanted to do the throat-cutting signal to stop her friend from talking.

'I can tell,' Sam said, his eyes sparkling eagerly as he squinted at Nova.

'She writes her own songs, too,' Gemma said.

Any chance of lightning striking me right now? Nova thought, looking up to the heavens. Clear and blazing sunshine. *No chance.*

'She's amazing!' Gemma was saying.

'Right,' Sam said, almost to himself. Then he looked intently at Nova and continued strumming. 'Come on, hit us with something of yours?'

'That's a hard no,' Nova said, shooting eye-daggers at Gemma, who shrugged and began rummaging in her handbag.

'Anyway, I'm going to go and grab a ginger beer from the truck,' Gem said, liberally applying some lip-gloss with her eyes trained on Otis. 'Want anything?'

'Actually, um, I was wondering if you have a little free time,' Sam asked, sounding a bit more tentative now. 'I'm headed over to the Lumina tent. They're having an open mic in like a half hour.' He looked at Nova. 'You want to come check it out? I won't make you sing, I promise,' he added.

'Err . . .' Nova began, then swallowed. 'I need to help with some clean up at the truck, so maybe—'

'She'll be there,' Gemma interjected quickly.

Sam chuckled, picking up his guitar and the last of his food. 'Awesome.' As he stood, he leaned down closer to Nova, and she could smell a light, spicy cologne coming from him. 'See you soon.'

Things were quiet when Nova and Gemma got back to the truck, though there was still the odd handful of people ordering food. Otis was heading out of the back as the girls arrived, tapping at his phone with one hand while untying his apron with the other. He looked up as he saw the girls approaching.

'Gem, I didn't know you liked Elmore Leonard,' he said, holding up his phone to show Gemma's latest Instagram post. She loved doing influencer-style videos, but with books reviews and bookshop hauls instead of fashion and beauty – even though Nova was sure she'd nail those too! But she'd had no idea Otis followed her friend on Instagram.

'Oh! Yeah,' Gemma replied, sounding a bit surprised about it herself. She actually seemed shy all of a sudden. 'My dad got me into him.'

'Nice,' Otis replied, smiling at her, and then he ambled off in the direction of the tents.

Nova headed into the truck and picked a couple of bottles of ginger beer out of the cooler. It was her mum's homemade recipe, potent with fiery ginger and cloves, and was delicious ice cold. But as she held out one of the bottles to Gemma, her friend seemed not to even notice. 'Uh earth to Gem, didn't you say you wanted one of these?' Nova asked.

'Hm? Oh no thanks, hon,' Gemma said distractedly, still looking in the direction Otis had gone. Nova smiled to herself, but for the first time she actually wondered if she *should* be trying to fix her brother and her best friend up? After all, who was better than Gem?

'Ooh, time-check, hon! We need to be getting you over to the Lumina tent!'

OK, maybe she wasn't so amazing after all. 'I dunno if I really want to go to that,' Nova said, taking a swig of her drink and replacing the bottle Gemma had rejected back into the cooler.

'Why not? That guy was *ridiculously* good looking and clearly into you, with zero ambiguity. Summer fling, remember?' she said, now reaching around Nova to fish the ginger beer out of the cooler again.

'You girls drinking up all our stock?' Nova's mum said with a smile, turning to look over her shoulder after handing some okra stew over to a couple of hungry-looking roadies through the serving hatch.

'Oh, do you need me to make up some more ginger beer?' Nova asked eagerly. Things must be

 85

desperate if she was actually *asking* for work!

'No, no, I think we're all right,' her mum replied. 'You girls go grab a couple of hours around the festival. Nova, I'll drop you a text if I need you, yeah? I'm going to start putting together the menu for Street to Elite.' She pulled out her trusty notebook and jotted down something. Nova knew that recipe ideas were her mum's equivalent of lyric ideas. Street to Elite was a really important food competition that offered funding for small food truck and pop-up restaurants to take their business to the next level. Nova's parents had got to the final round last year but missed out on the grand prize. This year they were going to give it everything they had.

'Great, thanks Aunty D,' Gemma was saying, beaming happily at Nova. 'Come on, hon, we're heading to that open mic. Live a little, eh?'

CHAPTER 7

Nova grudgingly linked arms with her friend, and they consulted the festival map on their phones to find the tent where Sam had said he was going. It was a bit out of the way, but when they got there the tent was really welcoming and warm. The floors were laid with rugs, and handfuls of people were lounging on them, looking up at the small stage. Although it was still bright sunshine outside, inside the tent was dark, with fairy lights strung up all around, and the distinctive scent of sandalwood. The smell reminded Nova of the joss sticks the Rastafarians outside Brixton station would burn while selling incenses and oils from their tables (if the police didn't give them hassle over it). She felt instantly at home, even if there was a funny, nervous feeling in the pit of her stomach, too.

'Signing up for the open mic, ladies?' a girl in a long, velvet dress and a pixie cut asked hopefully, proffering a clipboard.

Nova quickly said, 'No, no, we're just here to watch.'

Gem looked slightly disappointed, but like always, didn't push Nova on her reluctance to perform her songs. Instead, she waved enthusiastically as she spotted Sam waiting off to the side of the stage with the other performers who'd signed up. Nova and Gemma sat down on one of the rugs near the front. They endured a painfully tuneless girl on a ukulele, and a boy wearing the Official Red Beanie of the Poet (as Gemma called it), who did some passable if overly earnest spoken word. Then Sam was called up to the stage.

'Next up,' the girl in the velvet dress said, standing on tiptoes to reach the microphone as she read off her clipboard, 'We have, uh . . . Sam Rodriguez. Give Sam a hand, guys!'

The audience gave a smattering of applause as Sam bounded on to the stage with his guitar. 'Hey. *¿Qué vola?*' he said, his deep voice resonating through the speakers and into Nova's chest. He looked around the space a bit, and when his eyes fell on Nova, his face broke into a wide grin. 'Pleasure to be here,' he continued, 'glad you could make it.' He was addressing the audience, but the comment seemed especially for her. Beside Nova, Gemma whooped and whistled. He adjusted a secondary microphone towards his guitar, wincing a little as feedback whined out of the speakers, but then gave a confident nod as he strummed the strings to make sure it was in tune. He began plucking the strings, playing the introduction to an upbeat song. 'This one's called "Winning You Around",' he said, meeting Nova's eye again and winking at her. Even though he was playing acoustic, it had a funky, Latin feel, and he added percussion on the body of his guitar. He was kind of like a much, much cooler Ed Sheeran, somehow making one guitar sound like a whole band.

Nova had to fight to keep her jaw from dropping, or from descending into astonished laughter. She was a strange mess of emotions – shock at Sam's brazenness, amazement at how fantastic his voice was, amusement at the humour of his lyrics about bumping into a girl who was 'hotter than a goat curry', and admiration at the smatterings of Spanish he added into them. And reluctance to let any of this actually be true, because of how adamant she was about not wanting to get into any kind of new romantic relationship. But . . . Sam's song was clearly all about her!

What is he doing?

Winning her over . . . ?

The audience absolutely lapped it up. Gemma was clapping along enthusiastically by the second chorus, as was everyone around them. A shaft of sunlight flashed into the tent as some of the people outside came to see what the cheering was about.

'Oh my gosh, babe,' Gemma said over the noise of the music. 'He is *smitten*!' She cackled, still clapping along. 'And he's really good, too, don't lie. Doesn't his voice remind you of someone? I can't quite put my finger on who . . .'

Nova didn't reply, she just watched as Sam finished the song with a humorous flourish on his guitar, to rapturous final applause.

'Hope you liked that one,' he said into the mic. It seemed like a statement, but again he was aiming it in Nova's direction. And it almost sounded more like a question, since she was the only one not clapping and whooping. She couldn't help it though. She wasn't quite sure *how* to react to Sam or his song. Part of her wanted to be happy and charmed, but another part, deeper down, felt like this was all just a preamble to more heartache.

'So yeah, my name is Sam Rodriguez. I've actually just set up an Insta page for my music, so if you could do me a solid and give me a follow, it's @SamRodriguezMusic, pretty easy to remember.' He chuckled. '*Muchas gracias*. Thank you!' He glanced back at Nova, looking a little bit less confident than he had before, and made his way off the stage. The velvet girl returned to the mic, still clapping.

'Wow, do as he says, guys, give him a follow – and remember you saw him here at Lumina first!'

As the young woman introduced the next act, Nova felt Gemma nudge her and turned to see a slight, concerned frown on her friend's face. 'What's up, Nov?'

Nova moved to stand up, keen to head out of the tent before Sam caught up with them. 'Err, nothing,' she mumbled. She sighed with relief as she felt her phone vibrate in her pocket, and pulled it out with a flourish. As she suspected, it was her mum, saying that Nova was needed back at the truck to help out. She flashed her screen at Gemma with an apologetic shrug. 'I've got to get back to the truck.'

Gemma didn't seem massively convinced, but

said, 'OK, hon. Well, I'm going to go and catch up with those girls I met yesterday. I might stick around for a sec and tell your friend Sam well done, though,' she added pointedly.

Nova nodded, quickly turning towards the exit. 'Cool. Err, yeah, tell him that from me, too. Sorry, got to run.' She ignored Gemma shaking her head as she walked quickly out, feeling a weird mixture of guilt and self-preservation.

CHAPTER 8

It was heading towards midnight by the time the queue at Eats & Beats finally dwindled enough for Nova's mum and dad to call it a night. Nova was helping her dad package up some of the ingredients they hadn't used to put into refrigeration ready for the final full day of the festival tomorrow when she heard her brother saying, 'All right, mate? Back again?' to someone through the serving hatch. 'Sorry, we're just packing up for the night. I can sort you out with some patties though . . .'

'Thanks, man. I, uh, I was actually wondering

if Nova was around?' The voice – and the accent – were unmistakeable. Nova straightened up and peered warily through the hatch to see Sam looking up at her.

'I've got this, Ots,' she said, taking the patties her brother had just finished warming up and putting them into one of their recycled brown paper bags. Otis raised an eyebrow at her, but moved aside so that she could make her way out the back of the truck to bring the food to Sam.

'Hi,' she said with a bit of a croak in her voice, and not just because of how exhausted she was. Nova had been feeling guilty ever since she'd fled the tent after Sam's performance. She was still sure that she wasn't interested in any kind of fling with him, but after him going to the trouble of actually writing her a song, it wasn't great of her to have left without at least saying thank you. She knew how vulnerable songwriting made you, after all. She could hardly imagine performing her own songs the way he had.

During her short breaks over the dinnertime

95

rush, she'd checked out his Instagram account. What she had seen there didn't make it any easier to convince herself she wasn't interested. Sam had posted a series of self-filmed videos performing his songs and one or two covers – including an Amy Winehouse tune. In all of the videos, he was self-effacing, charming, and almost painfully good-looking. There were a few selfies that ranged from goofy to thirst-trapping, and some envy-inducing shots of palm trees and the ocean from his life in Miami. She'd watched one video of him having just woken up, tousle-haired and topless, playing a song he claimed had come into his head as a dream an embarrassing number of times. Nova had concentrated extra hard not to accidentally 'like' any of the posts, but her attraction to Sam made it all the more important. The more rational part of her brain was telling her that she should find a way not to let him get the wrong idea with her. Until now, she'd thought rushing off without saying goodbye earlier could have done just that, but here he was, back at the truck. At least since he was here, she had the chance to let him down more easily and to apologise face to face. She moved away from the glow of the food truck into a darker, quieter area where her family were less likely to earwig.

'I'm glad you're here,' she said. Sam's expression seemed to brighten, making her feeling bad all over again. 'Look, sorry about having to run earlier. My mum needed me. But, um, you did really well.'

He was wearing a dark zip-up hoodie and well-worn jeans, as the night had brought a slight chill to the air. Nova was still in her yellow vest-top because working in the truck was always hot, but she felt goosebumps prickle her arms now. It might have been the temperature, but it might also have been just how good Sam looked, even though his expression was wry.

'I did really well, huh? You know, you need to dial down your enthusiasm a little there, Nova Clarke.'

Nova sighed, smiling a little bit. 'OK, fine. You

were amazing,' she capitulated honestly, and he grinned at her. Nova folded her arms around herself – to stay warm but also, maybe subconsciously, to protect herself. 'Look, Sam, I'm really flattered at this attention and everything, but I don't think—'

'Don't think,' Sam interjected, his face serious now. 'Don't think,' he repeated. 'I do like you, Nova. I know I don't know you, but I do know I like you. We've got one more evening here. The festival ends day after tomorrow, and there's no telling what might happen after that. But . . . how about you just give me that one evening and don't think?'

His voice was lower now, and Nova shivered involuntarily as he moved a little bit closer, looking down at her with a mixture of hope and undeniable attraction. Was he really this into her? Nova started to let that tiny voice in her head chime in, beginning to convince her. Sam wasn't even from the UK – he'd be back to the States at some point soon, so there was no danger of falling for him.

Spending the last evening of the festival with him could be fun, a way to shake off her old romantic demons. After all, that's why they called it a rebound, right? Her mum had already said she and Otis could have the final night of the festival off to enjoy themselves while she went to watch Hector's band. Nova had planned to just hang out with Gemma, but she had a feeling her friend would support this decision.

Don't think . . .

'OK,' she whispered.

Sam gave her that devastating smile. 'I'm sorry, what was that?'

'OK.'

He cupped one ear jokingly, and she rolled her eyes.

'Yes,' she said.

He made an exaggerated double-fisted salute up to the starry night sky, then looked at Nova again. 'Get some rest. I'll see you tomorrow evening, seven o'clock, in front of the helter-skelter.' Sam looked at her a beat longer, then put his hands in his jeans pockets, turned on his heel and walked away, calling over his shoulder, 'You'll have zero regrets, Nova Clarke.'

CHAPTER 9

'OK. OK. Wow. OK. Mate. Like, where to start? Wow.'

Nova laughed as she watched Gemma almost short-circuit both with the information she'd given her about Sam asking her out, but also about the vast limitations of the clothing she'd brought with her. It was the mid-morning quiet point in the demand at the food truck, and so Gem had dragged Nova back to her tent to strategise about what to wear on her date that night. Everything she'd packed was laid out on the inflatable mattress inside her tent, and Gemma was shaking her head in despair. Even the sparkly top that her friend had bought was off limits until she could get it to a dry cleaner back home – and besides, Gemma said, 'Babe, we cannot be out here repeating outfits for such a momentous occasion.'

Nova had tried to emphasise just how *un*-momentous this occasion was, but even she had to admit she was a tiny bit excited about that evening. Fine, more than a tiny bit.

'Gem, I'm sure he won't really care what I'm wearing,' she tried, and Gemma turned from the pair of frayed denim shorts she was studying to fix Nova with a stare.

'Nova, that is not the point of getting dressed up. You dress for *you*—' she tapped the centre of her chest earnestly as she spoke '—so that you're feeling your absolute and most fabulous, inside *and* out! You get me?'

Nova bit her lip to hide a laugh, but she was kind of motivated by Gemma's sincerity. Her friend was right – looking good *did* make her feel good. That was part of why she dismissed it (or more like, was ready to go toe to toe!) when people called Gem shallow. The girl's commitment to beauty and fashion went much deeper than the surface.

'I get you, hon,' Nova told her, even though the question had been rhetorical.

'And I've *got* you, Nov. I'll be back here at five-thirty with options. Operation Festival Fling is a go!' She bent to make her way out of the flap in the tent, looking extremely determined.

Nova shook her head as she watched her friend go, but she knew Gemma just wanted her to have some fun.

After tidying up, Nova stepped out into the warmth of another sunny summer day. As she made her way through the festival site to the food trucks, Nova had to admit she kept scanning every tall and tanned boy in case it was Sam. It was only one evening, she knew, but she wondered if there might be a teeny-tiny possibility that Sam *was* different. He had a totally different vibe from Nate, that was for sure. He was confident, but she couldn't imagine anyone describing him as arrogant in the way they might her ex. He was funny, and his charm didn't seem contrived. And he was definitely *more* than easy on the eye, but again in a much less self-conscious way than Nate was. Nova knew that comparing the two boys was a pointless exercise, but she couldn't help it. She even found herself humming one of the tunes Sam had posted on his page as she headed back to the truck.

Get a grip, Nova. This is just one evening of fun!

As she arrived back at the food truck, her mum and dad had their backs turned to her, hunched over the small stove. They each dipped a spoon inside a simmering pot.

'I think maybe some brown sugar?' Hector said, though he sounded unsure.

Nova's mum smacked her lips together lightly, tasting again. 'You think?' She whipped out a fresh spoon – double-dipping was a no-no – and took another bit of the stew out of the pot. 'Maybe.

Ah! Nov! We've been playing around with this aubergine curry for goodness knows how long. We can't tell if it's working any more. Taste!'

Nova was more than happy to – it smelled delicious! She had a spoonful. 'It's perfect. Seriously!'

Her dad looked pleased, and her mum scribbled a final note in her book, then said, 'Hec, I think we're there, you know! This competition might actually be ours this time . . .'

Nova knew why her mum's voice held so much hope. The competition was prestigious, and winning the prize money would mean a whole new era for Eats & Beats. Maybe even that after this season, Nova might be able to just go to festivals without working at them!

She got to work helping to prep for the start of the dinner rush, glad of the distraction from thinking about her sort-of-date with Sam. Nova was almost surprised when she saw Gemma heading towards the truck a bit later, bumping an impractical wheeled suitcase across the dried-out grass. She glanced at her watch and realised it was half past five already. When she looked back up, though, Nova noticed that Gemma had come to a halt, and she and Otis were standing off to one side chatting. She was doubly surprised when she saw her brother handing over a book to Gemma, which her friend took while nodding and smiling, seeming genuinely interested.

Hmm . . . !

Gemma tucked the book into the leather backpack she was carrying, and waved as she spotted Nova.

'Dad, am I all right to head off now?' she asked. Her dad swung his thick locs out of the way over one shoulder as he gave Nova a one-armed squeeze.

'Course, darling. Have a great time tonight, yeah? And remember to check in with us, you hear?'

'I will. Hope the gig goes amazingly later!'

Nova felt a rush of relief, excitement and nerves as she bounded down the little metal steps out of the food truck to meet Gemma. They hugged, and Gem crinkled her nose a bit.

'Babe, I hate to break it, but you smell of fried food and spices. Don't get me wrong, I'm definitely looking forward to getting my fix of E&B grub in a bit, and we know Mr Rodriguez is a fan, too. *However*, I'm not sure he's going to be into his date smelling like a caff . . .'

Nova knew her friend was right, but the thought of facing the showers again made her sigh in anguish. They were bad enough first thing in the morning when they'd supposedly been cleaned! Still, she braved a quick wash and then headed back to her tent, ready to get the full makeover treatment from Gemma.

But when she arrived, Nova couldn't help overhearing a phone call her friend was on, and paused outside so she didn't interrupt.

'Mum, I'm not sure if she's going to be there. He hasn't mentioned anything to me yet, but believe me, I'm not into the idea of having to hang out with some new woman, either.' Nova heard Gem give a long sigh. 'I'd rather it was just me and

Dad, too. Anyway, listen, I've got to go, OK? Love you, Mum . . . Yep . . . Bye.'

Nova gave it a moment before opening the tent flap and moving slowly inside to sit next to Gemma on her mattress. She was looking at her phone contemplatively, but gave Nova a wide, slightly forced smile when she came in. Nova nudged her with one shoulder.

'Mum getting the fear about your dad dating other people?' she asked.

Gemma let out a scoffing sound. 'Babe, I told you, I have a feeling he started up with that before he and Mum even properly split up.' She looked at Nova with a mixture of anger and sadness.

Nova raised her eyebrows, biting her lip in sympathy. 'Yeah. Sorry, I couldn't help hearing a bit of your call. It must be hard feeling like they're putting you in the middle of the two of them,' she began tentatively.

Gem shrugged, looking unsure. 'A bit, yeah. I know it's been years, but sometimes I wish . . .'

'They'd just get back together again?' Nova finished.

Gemma nodded. 'I mean, that isn't going to happen, I know that. I just kind of wish my mum could move on, too, you know?'

Nova reached around to rub her friend's back. 'I hear that, Gem. I suppose it's hard for her, having been cheated on. I know it's nowhere near the same thing, but I can relate!'

'Hah! Innit! Thanks, hon. I should go easier on her.' Gemma smiled at her wryly.

'Well, know I'm here for you no matter what, yeah?'

'Course,' Gemma said with another smile, then she drew in a breath. 'Anyway, let's get back to the matter at hand!' She stood up, stooping a little due to the height of the tent, and gestured theatrically to the outfits she'd laid out on the bed. Nova immediately vetoed two of them, and then studied the simple black dungaree-style shift dress with gold fastenings that caught her eye.

'Ooh, this is a bit of me,' she said. Gemma

109

rolled her eyes, but held up some chunky gold costume jewellery.

'Thought you might say that. But we shall *accessorise*?'

Half an hour later, Nova was dressed and Gemma was finishing off her make-up with a slick of red lipstick.

'Oh. Yass. Nineties Versace vibes!' Gemma exclaimed, sitting back to admire her handiwork.

Nova had piled her locs into a bun on top of her head, and the girls emerged out of the tent so Gem could take some pictures for her to scrutinise the full-length look. She had on her favourite chunky Doc Marten boots with the short dress so it didn't look too over the top.

'Nice one, G. This is actually a great look,' Nova said with a grin, studying the photos on her friend's screen.

'Sure I can't persuade you to make a quick pit-stop at the glitter dust tent, really get the festival aesthetic happening?' Gemma asked.

'Uh, nope! Told you, do you have any idea

what that stuff does to the environment? I heard they're stopping it from next year anyway, I signed the petition and—'

Her friend held up her hands, chuckling. 'OK, OK, protect our oceans. Just a thought!'

Checking her own phone, Nova realised it was already ten to seven. 'Wow, I'd better get going if I'm going to get across the site to the helter-skelter on time,' she said, feeling nervous butterflies begin to take flight in the centre of her stomach. Even more so when Gemma gave a squeal of excitement. 'Remember, it's just a bit of fun, yeah? Don't start planning your bridesmaid outfit!' Nova said to her friend, who nodded faux-sombrely.

'Course. Yep. Just a bit of fun. But make sure you actually have some, yeah? You deserve, after the nonsense with he-whose-name-shall-not-be-mentioned. OK? Promise me you'll enjoy yourself and not overthink things?'

It was Nova's turn to nod. 'I promise,' she said, though she knew deep down it was harder to guarantee. She made Gemma give her one last lipstick-on-teeth check. 'Right. I should head off, then,' she said, grabbing her mini-backpack. She hesitated, though, feeling glued to the spot. Gem gripped her shoulders and spun her around, pointing her in the direction she needed to head across the festival site, and gave her a joking push.

'The minute you get back, I want you on that phone providing me with Every. Single. *Second* of detail, yeah?' she called after Nova.

'Yup!'

Right, Nova thought, *one evening of fun, here I come!*

CHAPTER 10

Nova felt her throat growing steadily drier as she approached the fairground attractions on the far side of the festival site. Part of her was worried Sam would stand her up, or that the whole evening would turn out to be some kind of painfully embarrassing disaster. But as she reached the helter-skelter, she spotted him.

Sam's back was to her, and he was wearing black jeans and a casual long-sleeved white shirt with the sleeves rolled up slightly, revealing his strong-looking forearms. In his hands, he seemed to be carrying something which, as Nova slowly got closer, she realised was a small, gift-wrapped package. There were swarms of people excitedly heading to the rides, and the clashing sounds of music and mechanics was almost deafening. Nova could see that Sam was scanning the crowds, and he looked a bit anxious. Glancing at her watch, she realised she was eight minutes late, and felt bad. Maybe he thought *she* was standing *him* up!

Quickening her pace, she sidled up behind him and tapped him on the shoulder. He spun around, and she couldn't help a grin at the relieved look on his face.

'Wow. Nova Clarke, you were worth the wait,' he said, taking her in from top to toe.

Nova hoped the sheen of sweat she felt prickle her forehead at his compliments wasn't too noticeable. 'You look pretty good yourself,' she told him, and he brushed off one shoulder jokingly.

'Thank you, thank you. Oh, this is for you. I figured flowers would be a little impractical,' he said, pushing his curls back with a sheepish look. He handed her the package, which was wrapped

114

in newspaper with a little bit of ribbon around it.

'Recycled packaging, eh?' she asked teasingly.

'The best kind, right?' he said.

'Actually, yeah. I'm all for doing what I can for the environment,' she offered, then pulled on the ribbon. They were still standing below the helter-skelter, but she'd almost tuned out everyone else around them – especially with the way that Sam was looking at her so appreciatively. She tucked the ribbon into the pocket of his hoodie, and pulled away the newspaper to reveal a . . .

'*Dictaphone*,' she read on the box. 'Err . . . thanks?'

Sam chuckled. 'It's a portable recorder. I don't know about you, but I hate how much memory gets used up on my phone when I have an idea I need to get down.' He looked at her, his smile a little less sure now. 'Uh, I thought you might feel the same way, with your songwriting and whatnot? They were doing some promotional thing near where I'm staying, so I grabbed one . . .'

Nova stared down at the gift, genuinely touched.

'This is really cool,' she said softly, then looked up into Sam's eyes. He stared down at her for what felt like ages, before clearing his throat.

'Glad you like it,' he said. 'And I'm hoping you're going to like what I've got planned for us tonight.'

Tucking the Dictaphone into her backpack, Nova smiled. 'I hope so too!'

Sam laughed his musical laugh, and pointed up above them at the helter-skelter. 'Well, first up, I've always wanted to try one of these things,' he said. 'What do you say?'

Nova doubted she'd have too much objection to anything Sam suggested when he looked at her with that smile. 'Yeah, why not?'

He stood aside and swept an arm towards the entrance. Given that there were much more exciting-looking rides, like the rickety but fun roller coaster, there wasn't much of a queue for the helter-skelter. A bored-looking older man took four pounds from Sam, and they began to climb up the metal stairs in the centre of the structure.

It was taller than it seemed from the ground, and Nova feigned panting and wiping her brow as they rounded yet another spiral of the staircase. But when they reached the top, there was a window looking out over the whole of the festival site.

'Wow, look at that. It's beautiful,' Nova said, then held her breath as she felt Sam move close beside her.

'Yeah,' he said, his voice low. His green eyes shone in the reflection of the twinkling lights outside as he looked directly at her.

Get moving, Nova . . .

She stepped away and grabbed a mat. 'Let's do this!' she said, a bit over-enthusiastically. She headed out to the top of the slide and flopped the mat down, settling on to it and pulling her dress down a bit, then smiled back up at Sam as he stood over her with his own mat. Taking a breath, she launched herself down the spiralling slide, giggling like a little girl. This silly ride, and being there with Sam, was making her feel freer than she had in a very long time.

As she reached the bottom of the ride, her head spinning, she heard Sam rushing down the slide behind her. His mat collided with hers, and she felt his hands touch her shoulders to steady himself, sending tingles down her arms as his warmth enveloped her.

'Who needs a roller coaster, huh?' he said, standing up and offering her a hand.

'Mmm,' Nova replied as he pulled her up, still buzzing from the contact. She didn't trust herself to say much more, especially when he didn't let go of her hand as they made their way out of the exit to the ride. As they passed a coconut shy with huge stuffed animals of various types hanging above it as prizes, Sam came to a halt.

'Oh, perfecto. We have to go full cliché here,' he told Nova. 'Plus, I already know how much you love hauling oversized stuff around, right?' He rolled his sleeves up more as Nova laughed, trying not to feel too bad about the fact he had to let go of her hand to do so. He bought five of the balls, and with a wink at Nova, he launched them at the coconuts.

And . . . completely failed to hit any of them.

They were both in hysterics as each ball whistled past its target.

'Wait, wait, this is clearly a job for a woman,' she said, taking her bag off her back and looking over her shoulder at him.

'*¡Tremenda manguita!*' he murmured with a smile.

Nova flushed. She didn't know what it meant, but the tone suggested something teasing but appreciative. She handed over her money to the woman running the stall, who nodded in solidarity. Five balls knocked with pleasing thwacks against the coconuts, sending them flying. All those days in the park at the cricket nets with her dad pretending she was bowling for the Windies had clearly worked out for her! Nova turned around, hands in the air, and did a jig. Sam stepped forward and smacked palms with her, his face so close she had to look away. She covered by stepping back to do an exaggerated bow, then began to

119

study the stuffed animals.

'Let's see,' she said, mockingly putting her fingers to her chin. 'Ooh! This one!' She pointed to an enormous pink elephant, and laughed mercilessly as the woman handed it straight to Sam, whose expression was a mixture of amused, awestruck and dismayed.

'I feel like I've been hustled,' he said, stuffing the toy under his arm.

Nova picked up her bag, still smiling gloatingly at him. They began to wander away from the fairground area, with Sam shaking his head ruefully. Walking past the vast city of tents set up in the distance, Nova whistled.

'I'm definitely glad I'm not trying to locate where I'm staying amongst all of that,' she said. 'Is that where you've been camping?'

Sam was looking away towards the tents still, and didn't seem in a hurry to meet her eye again. 'Nah, I've been staying with my dad . . .'

'Oh, right,' Nova replied, nodding. 'The roadies and stuff must have their own area like we do for the catering.'

'Mmm hmm.' Sam readjusted the elephant, then finally did look at Nova again, with a glint in his eye. 'Anyway, look, so if we were back in Miami I'd be taking you to my favourite spot for some grub. But since we're here, and you're already familiar with my favourite place to eat *here*, I'm guessing you'd like to try something different?'

'Uh, yeah,' Nova told him. The very idea of heading back to Eats & Beats to have her parents scrutinise Sam was a definite no-no.

'OK, well I know neither of us are vegan, but I've heard really good things about this place,' he said, gesturing to one of the lone food trucks that were dotted sporadically away from the main area where her family's truck was located. There was a small queue, but Nova was willing to wait.

'Oh yeah, The Wow Burger! I've heard of these guys. It's supposed to taste just like meat, but without the environmental impact, right?' They joined the line and Nova scanned the menu, getting hungrier by the moment. 'I've been cutting way back on my red meat, so this sounds really good.'

'You're really into the whole "saving the planet" thing, right?' Sam sounded somewhat wry, and Nova frowned a little.

'Well, yeah, climate change is a fact, and we need to do something about it pretty sharpish or we won't have a planet left.' She cringed at how defensive she sounded, but it really did mean a lot to her. 'I actually reckon that's the field I want to work in.'

Sam squinted his eyes at her. 'Really? Science, huh? I figured you as a musician.'

Oh. 'You haven't even heard anything I've written,' she mumbled, but something about him telling her that felt meaningful.

He shrugged. 'Sure, but sometimes you can just get a sense, you know?'

Nova turned to study him in the light from the food truck. He'd settled the elephant between his legs as he stood over it, and she smiled at the comical image. Sam was someone she had to admit she wanted to get a better sense of, too. In lots of ways he seemed fun and open, but she couldn't shake the feeling that there might be something he was hiding. Was it just her paranoia about avoiding getting too close to anyone? She wasn't sure. 'So is music something you're looking to do full time?' she asked, watching his eyes light up.

'Totally,' he said, and then his face grew a bit more serious. 'I just want to make sure it's . . . on my own terms, you know?'

She wasn't sure she did know, and she was about to ask what he meant, when the young woman inside the truck with a red apron, a red face and red hair quickly enquired what they wanted to order. Nova knew how busy she was, so she didn't dither about telling Sam what she'd like to eat. He ordered that, plus what seemed to Nova like a flashy amount of extra food, swiping his card without even looking at the total.

'You know it's just the two of us, right?' she asked jokingly, and he looked down at her, amused.

'I figure we should support people trying to do the environment a solid, right? Plus those onion rings looked bangin'.' He grabbed the bag of food and led them away to a quieter spot underneath a tree. They sat down, and Nova smiled as he positioned the stuffed elephant behind her back against the tree's trunk so she could lean on it.

'Why, thank you, Nelly,' she said.

'You've named her?'

'What makes you think it's a girl?'

Sam smiled too, and began to munch on his burger, pulling an appreciative face as he tasted it. Nova bit into hers, too, careful not to make a mess or get ketchup anywhere. It really did taste like meat! 'Thanks a lot for this, Sam,' she said, earnestly. 'I mean, not just the burger. It's been nice to get to enjoy the festival a bit.'

He watched as she picked at some fries. 'For sure. I'm just glad you said yes,' he said softly. 'Anyway, the night is young – we should go check out some of the stages after we finish eating. And hey, I still want to know more about your songwriting. I'm not letting that drop. Thought you could distract me with . . . talk of saving

Mother Earth?' One side of his mouth quirked up. Nova took a long sip of her Coke, trying not to blush.

'It's just something I do for me, really. I do love writing music, but I don't think it's massively realistic as a career – for me, anyway. I mean, it was my dad's dream to be a famous musician, and he's ended up running a restaurant. He still makes music on the side, and I know it hurts, not having found the success he wanted. My parents are keen for me to stick to academic stuff, and I get it. I don't want to end up disappointed.' She drew a breath, surprised at how honest she was being. 'Besides, mortification is the first thing I feel whenever I try and perform my own stuff in front of anyone.' She did a mock shiver and took another bite of her food.

Sam wiped his hands on a napkin, shaking his head. 'I don't know . . . It's possible to be really successful at music.' He was still looking down at his hands, with an odd expression on his face – something between a smile and a frown. 'You just have to be doing it for the right reasons. Because you really love it, you know. And from the way you're talking about it I can tell that you do,' he said, looking at her now. 'I do, too. There's nothing else like it, right?' He nudged her with one shoulder, but didn't move back away afterwards. Nova saw Sam's eyes move down towards her mouth, and her heart rate began to climb. But he reached down for another napkin and dabbed it on one corner of her lips.

'Had a little sauce there,' Sam said, his eyes still flicking between her mouth and her eyes.

She gave a nervous titter and broke his gaze. 'Err, thanks.' *Nice one, Nova.*

They finished their food, and she pulled out her phone to check the festival app and see who was due on which stage. She quickly closed the numerous messages of encouragement from Gemma before Sam could see them as he looked over her shoulder.

'Ooooh, Flightpath are about to get on the main stage,' she said sarcastically, scrunching her nose up. Sam was quiet though, and she turned to look at him. 'Oh God, they're not, like, your favourite band or something, are they?' she asked, only half-jokingly, but it took him a second before he flashed her a smile.

'Oh, for sure,' he said, then whipped her phone out of her hands to study the app. She watched anxiously, hoping Gem didn't decide now was a perfect time to send another embarrassing message. 'Hmm, let's see . . . Ah! I've got it.' He handed her phone back with a cunning expression on his face. 'Grab your stuff, Clarke. Nelly, good sir?' Sam threw away their rubbish, then picked up the elephant with one hand and offered Nova the other again to help her up. And again, he didn't let go as they began to walk, gripping it tighter as he glanced over at her.

'Where are we heading?' Nova asked, hoping desperately that her palm didn't start to sweat.

'It's a surprise,' Sam told her mysteriously. They reached a smaller stage that was decorated with palm trees and twinkling white lights, where a slightly older woman with long thin dreadlocks a bit like Nova's was dressed in dark, flowing clothes. She was holding a violin, on which she played a soothing, slow introduction before speaking in to the microphone.

'My name is Sonta,' she said, 'thanks for coming to check me out.' The crowd rippled with applause and a few whoops and whistles, and Nova's breath caught as the woman began to sing. It was a haunting, beautiful melody, something between jazz and folk.

'Wow,' Nova said, looking over to Sam, who to her surprise was singing along. He turned to her with a smile.

'She's amazing, isn't she?' he said, leaning close so that he didn't disrupt the people around them, swaying to her music. Nova nodded enthusiastically, enraptured. 'I read an interview with her online a couple weeks ago, and she was talking about her stage fright,' he said. 'But look what we'd be missing out on if she didn't overcome it to perform her songs.' He grinned pointedly at Nova.

'OK, OK, you might be right.'

It felt weird that Sam was so convinced her music was even *worth* working on overcoming her hesitance, but it also made her feel a warm glow inside – as did Sonta's performance. They focussed their attention fully on the stage as her band came out to join her, launching into a few more upbeat songs. As they listened and watched, the musicians moved into a slower tune. Nova felt Sam edging closer to her and, taking a breath, he seemed to make a decision to put one arm around her shoulders. Feeling the warmth of Sam's body, Nova instinctively settled into his side and let him move them gently to the music. It felt . . . right. She was only jolted out of her reverie as Sonta gave one final long note on her violin, and then thanked the audience, who gave her a long and rapturous round of applause.

'That was *incredible*!' Nova said, joining in.

'Yeah,' Sam replied softly, looking at her.

Trying to break the tension, Nova smiled a little

and began to move away from the stage as some techs started setting up for the next band.

'OK, next destination is my choice,' she said, skipping backwards as Sam followed her.

He held Nelly the Elephant's trunk up close to his face and asked him, 'What do we make of this, *acere*? Do we trust her?'

Nova couldn't keep the amusement from her face. Checking the site map to make sure she was taking them in the right direction, she gestured for Sam to follow her as she headed towards a circus-style red-and-white striped tent a few feet away. The area was strangely quiet – and Nova knew why. As they headed for the entrance, she smiled at the friendly woman handing her a pair of wireless headphones, and another pair to Sam as he sidled up behind Nova. All around them, others were wearing the headphones, too, with their hands in the air, jumping up and down, and beaming at each other as they danced in silence.

'Uh, OK . . .' Sam began, but Nova put her finger over her lips to shush him before slipping on the headphones and indicating he should do the same.

Immediately, a pounding rhythm was in her ears and she began to shimmy in time to it, laughing as Sam put his on and raised his eyebrows. Wordlessly, he began to dance too, matching Nova's movements and jokingly flapping Nelly's ears along with the beat for a moment before setting the elephant down next to them and moving a bit closer. The music was a thumping mixture of afrobeats and house, and Nova couldn't resist really getting into it, especially as she watched Sam, who was apparently also a fantastic dancer on top of everything else. He moved behind her and swayed with the rhythm. Nova couldn't tell if the electric feeling was the heat of the dancing and the sweating bodies around them, or the fact that he was so close, with one hand resting on her hip as they moved. Time flew by as they danced. He swung her around, and the dancers around them pressed in. She was forced so close to Sam that he had to reach forward to steady her.

As he did, they both simultaneously stopped

moving, despite the jostling people around them. With his hands warm on her shoulders, Nova watched as Sam leaned down towards her, a half-smile on his lips, his green eyes sparkling in the flashing disco lights. She couldn't help but stare. Her breath quickened and her heart began pulsing even faster though she had stopped dancing. The music in her headphones seemed to match it, and she took a risk and moved in closer. Was she actually going to let him kiss her? The logical part of her brain wanted her to stop it, but she felt almost powerless to resist . . .

Then an overenthusiastic blonde girl with her hair in bunches stumbled into Nova, pushing her awkwardly into Sam's shoulder, and he tripped backwards over the oversized stuffed elephant and fell on to his bum, laughing. Nova almost went over too, but managed to steady herself, her own laughter a mixture of relief and genuine mirth. She did, however, drop her phone out of her dress pocket, and as she retrieved it from being trampled under the feet of dancing festival-goers, she noticed it was already half past midnight.

'Whoa,' she said, staring at the messages from her mum not-so-subtly reminding her that she had a midnight curfew. She pulled off her headphones, as Sam did the same. Her ears rang at the sudden change in volume. 'I'd better be heading,' she said regretfully, holding her hand out to pull him up. The tent was getting packed as the performers on the main stages around the site finished their sets. 'This was really fun, Sam.' She meant it – it was actually one of the best nights she'd had . . . well, ever. But as people impatiently pushed into the tent, it was harder for the two of them to stay close together.

'I can walk you—' Sam began, frowning as two beer-drinking lads started doing an exaggerated dance around him.

Nova sensed this was her chance. If she let Sam walk her back to her tent, she had a feeling the magic of the evening would sweep her away into forgetting her promise to herself. She just wanted to leave the night as a great memory, not as something that could eventually lead to heartbreak all over again.

'Uh, it's cool. I've got to run, I'm really sorry – my parents are going to be on a mad one if I'm much later.' She quickly called, 'Thanks a lot,' and let the crowd part them once and for all, trying to ignore the dejected look on Sam's face, and the sinking feeling in her chest.

PART II
Summer Fields

CHAPTER 11

The sound of the heavy patter of rain on the pavement came in relentlessly through the propped-open door of the café. Nova leaned her chin on her hand as she sat on a stool at the counter. Summer had apparently decided sunshine was passé, and Island Rocks felt like a million years ago now, even though it had only been a week since she got back to London. It was muggy as a swamp, hence the door being open, and still light outside despite the time heading for eight. At least, for once, she wasn't serving customers at Eats & Beats. Tonight, her job was minute-taking.

Her mum was holding her monthly Sunday night meeting of local women business-owners, and on the agenda tonight were Nova's ideas for a new green initiative in the area. Trouble was, she was barely able to concentrate – the last few nights had been sleepless, or filled with more dreams. This time, rather than just nightmares about her stupid ex, another face was occupying her nocturnal thoughts. *Sam Rodriguez.*

Nova couldn't stop thinking about the evening they'd shared at the festival, and about how much fun she'd had despite her desperate hope that she wouldn't get sucked in by his charms. Most of all, she was filled with regret at the disappointed look on his face when she left him at the silent disco – and the fact that she'd been so determined to get out of there that she hadn't even got his number, or given him hers.

She'd been trying to convince herself that was for the best, because the frequency with which she'd been checking his Instagram page was getting embarrassing. Just maybe, she'd been hoping Sam would have sought her out online, or posted some cryptic message on his own feed, or even another song about her. Heck, she'd half hoped that he'd turn up at the food truck the morning after their date while they were packing up, but no such luck. Of course, *she* could have sent him a private message on his social media, but something was holding her back. Not just her 'no boys' summer vow, but a feeling that if he wasn't the one to reach out, then it was a sign that she should just leave things be.

'We did hear back from the council on the recycling collections, Meg, yes. Nov, can you pull up the email they sent?' Deana was asking.

'Sorry?' She looked up, and was faced with a group of expectant middle-aged women. 'Oh, err, yeah, sorry. One sec.' She tried to avoid the look of curiosity on her mum's face. Ordinarily, given this golden opportunity to influence the environmental efforts of the community, Nova would have been fully engaged. She frowned at the laptop screen, annoyed at herself, and quickly found the email. 'It was about as unhelpful as you'd expect,' Nova told the group, smiling ruefully. 'They said they'll "consider" our proposal for an additional pickup. But I'm going to make sure to keep piling on the pressure. They can't expect us to be able to cope with the volume of waste that *truly* focussing on our recycling is going to generate. And I'm going to keep on at them in terms of accountability for where our waste is being taken, too.'

Nova's mum nodded, and gave her daughter a subtle wink. 'Great work, sweetheart.'

The meeting eventually came to an end, and the businesswomen broke into gossip and nibbling the snacks that Deana had made. Nova's eyes strayed back to her phone screen as it lit up on the counter next to her. She was very keen for her heart not to leap each time that happened, hoping it would be a message from Sam. It was a news alert from an app, but Nova smiled as she also noticed Gemma's name above a message.

Has your mum made those rice flour-banana dumpling thingies tonight? Don't lie to me. I'm already OMW.

The message was from fourteen minutes ago.

They're called akara kuru, Nova replied.

Nova wasn't surprised when she looked up from that very message to see Gemma already shaking out an umbrella in the doorway. She sniffed the air exaggeratedly, then frowned as she saw the group of businesswomen surrounding the snacks. Swooping towards the paper plates, Gemma loaded one up, scooped a mound of the delicious spicy tomato-and-onion mix that went with the akara kuru on to her plate, and then finally made her way over to Nova.

'Mmm. Hey, babe,' she said through a mouthful. 'All done with putting the world to rights?'

Nova swiped a dumpling, chuckling at Gemma's noise of protest as she munched and swallowed. 'You know, you'd do well to come to one of these meetings, G,' she told her friend.

Gemma pulled a face, then continued to chew blissfully.

'Err, by the way, love the 'do. Biting my style?' Nova asked, reaching up to touch one of Gemma's freshly installed crochet faux-locs, which were ombred from dark at the roots to honey blond at the tips. She knew her friend had ordered the pack from the States.

'Please, as if I could,' Gem said, flipping her new hair over her shoulder, and then waving to Nova's mum as she stood in the corner chatting to the woman who ran the grocer's across the road. Nova wanted to tell Gemma that she didn't need to always dismiss a compliment, but wasn't sure if it was the right time to bring it up.

'You look amazing, hon,' she said emphatically.

She was about to check on how things were going with Gemma's parents, when her friend's whole demeanour seemed to light up. Nova turned and saw that her brother had just come through the door of the café. Gemma wiped her mouth quickly with a napkin and smiled broadly – and to

Nova's surprise, Otis actually came over when he saw them sitting at the counter. Usually he'd scuttle up the stairs before their mum gave him a task, or one of the women asked him when he was getting married.

'Hey, Otis,' Gemma said, though for once her voice sounded a bit more normal and a bit less cooing.

'Hey,' he replied with a broad smile back, then he reached out to dap Nova quickly, in his customary manner. But even as their fists connected, she noticed her brother was more focussed on Gemma.

'So, here you go,' Gem was saying, pulling something from her bag. It was a chunky hardback – legendary music super-producer Quincy Jones' autobiography.

'Err, what's going on with these book club vibes?' Nova asked. 'And you know I love Q! How come you've never lent that to me?'

Otis took the book, still smiling at Gemma, and then nudged Nova in the shoulder. 'Jealousy is an ugly trait, sis.' *Was* she jealous? Gemma and her brother did seem to be getting on pretty well . . . Otis was studying the back cover, nodding. 'Yeah, this is sick. Nice one, Gem, really appreciate it.'

Gemma blushed a bit and shrugged. 'I saw from Otis' Insta story that he had watched a movie about his life,' she explained to Nova, 'so I just let him know we had this book knocking about on our shelves and that he might be into it. It was my dad's,' she said, her eyes clouding a bit, 'but he left it behind when he went . . . Anyway, it's been on the shelf for years, so I finally gave it a read. It's good. You can borrow it after, Nov.'

Nova glanced at Otis, who looked back at her with a similar concern in his eyes at Gemma's demeanour. To her surprise, her brother chimed in. 'Well, at least your dad left some good reading material, eh?' he said, giving Gemma a wink that even Nova had to admit was winning. 'I'll figure out a good read to lend you to repay the favour, yeah?'

Gemma brightened, especially when Otis

reached out and gave her shoulder a quick, consolatory rub before hiking his bag back on to his shoulder. 'Right. I'd better head, I told Kwesi I'd give him a thrashing on the PS4 tonight.'

Nova could often hear him even through her bedroom wall trash-talking on his head-mic while playing online computer games with his mates and complete strangers. It was annoying, but he'd earned some pretty strong brother points just now, so she'd let it slide tonight.

'Enjoy,' she said, chuckling as Gemma's eyes followed Otis all the way to the door up to their flat before returning to Nova.

'Oof,' Gemma said, holding her newly installed hair off her neck for a moment before letting it fall. 'It is a crying shame that Otis is your bro, so you can't fully back how much of a moment that was,' she said, and Nova pulled a face. Gemma ignored her. 'He's delish, babe. Face it. Anyway, what about your Cuban-American-Brit love interest, eh? Have you got up the guts to message him yet?'

'I don't need guts,' Nova replied in a mumble, turning towards her laptop to avoid Gemma's raised eyebrow. She pretended to be fascinated by an email from a shopping site. 'Ooh, what do you think about these?'

'*Those?*' Gemma's disgust made Nova laugh. 'No, no, no, babe. I know I'm not going to be there, but please tell me you're not going to be running around Summer Fields fest in some nasty vintage shorty overalls. *Tragique!* A cute onesie, I'd allow, but—'

'Relax, G,' Nova said, still chuckling. 'I'm not getting them.'

Gemma clocked Nova's amusement and rolled her eyes, smiling too. 'OK, but I'm thinking there's every possibility Sam the Loverman might be at this next festival too, right?'

The thought had crossed Nova's mind. About a hundred times. It was possible – after all, if Sam's dad *was* a roadie, he'd probably be working the whole circuit. Summer Fields was by far the biggest festival in the country. It sold out in minutes, as it did every year. But if Sam wasn't looking to reach out to her on socials, what were the odds he'd seek out the Eats & Beats truck again? Maybe he *was* completely put off by the way she legged it like Cinderella after their date, and he wanted nothing more to do with her. She couldn't blame him – and hadn't that been the desired effect, anyway?

Ugh, enough of thinking about this, Nova!

She sighed. 'He might be, yeah,' she said, 'but to be honest, I'd much rather you were going to be there.'

Gemma reached over and squeezed Nova's knee. 'God, me too. I mean, going to Mexico will be sick, but my dad left me a message earlier saying he wants to talk to me about something to do with the holiday. I'm thinking he's going to be inviting *that woman* to come with us.' She took a breath. 'Weirdness will abound, I'm sure of it.'

Nova placed her hand over Gem's sympathetically. 'Look, like you said, the place itself will be great, right? Virgin piña coladas on the beach, hot Mexican guys, time to read?' Nova felt a warm smile cross her face that it was the latter that made Gemma's eyes light up the most. 'Can't argue with that!'

'True say. And SF fest will be cool, too, hon.'

Nova was called away for a second by her mum asking her to explain one of their ideas to one of the local stall-holders from the market. When she returned, Gemma was scrolling through her phone.

'Ew, babe look at this,' she said, showing Nova her screen. 'Gas-guzzling PJ? How five years ago, right?'

A beautiful, familiar-looking woman was doing a video on the tarmac in front of a private jet.

'Sadie . . . Varma, right?'

Gemma applauded. 'Ah, my teachings are sinking in!'

'As are mine!' Nova joked, then realised that a celebrity she did know was lurking in the background of the shot. 'Oh, and is that what's-his-name from FlightPath?'

'Clay Cooper? Yeah, Sadie's been doing the

absolute *most* making sure everyone knows they're engaged now. It's like, we get it, you're about to be a kept woman or whatever.'

Nova sensed that Gemma was still loving the celeb gossip of it all. 'Like you say though, seems a bit hypocritical of him to bang on about being an eco-warrior when he's flying around in—' But Nova's words ran short. She had accidentally scrolled past the video, and down to the next post on Gemma's Instagram feed. It was a post from Nathan, and the image and caption made Nova freeze.

After searching for so long, and finding all the wrong ones, I can say this girl is the only girl who truly has my heart. Happy three month anniversary, baby!

The picture showed Nate and Amanda, faces pressed closely together, looking blissfully happy.

'What is it, hon?' Gemma asked, taking her phone back. 'Oh . . . Nov, I'm so sorry. I thought

I'd unfollowed him, I swear. I'm doing it right now. What a scumbag . . .'

Nova shook her head. 'It's fine.'

'It's not,' Gemma said sympathetically. 'Look, I reckon we could both use a gigantic bowl of your dad's rum ice cream and a night in front of Netflix.'

Nova drew in a cleansing breath and stood up from her stool. 'Sounds like a plan!'

CHAPTER 12

It had been three days since Nova's eyeballs had been assaulted with Nathan's picture on Instagram. As she lay in bed looking at her packed rucksack once again, ready to head to Summer Fields the next morning with her family, she began to think. Then she began to hum. Suddenly, lyrics began to form in her mind, and she sat up, her eyes falling on the box with the Dictaphone that Sam had given her. She'd been avoiding actually using it for fear that it would trigger more regretful thoughts in her mind, but when she was packing earlier, she had found it in the bottom of her bag. Now, she picked it up and shook the little machine out of its packaging. A quick glance at the instructions, and then she hit *record* and sang the beginnings of the song she'd just thought up. She pressed *stop* and then rewound to hear what she'd come up with so far. It wasn't bad, actually . . .

She slid off the bed and pulled her keyboard closer. She listened to the machine again, then found a new space on the tape to begin recording again, glad that her parents were still downstairs in the restaurant finishing up, and Otis was out with his mates. Before she knew it, she'd written a whole song about her heartache at seeing Nathan moving on – but also about having hope for the days to come. If she was honest, that part was because of the possibility that, someway, somehow, she might encounter Sam again at the festival.

Satisfied, Nova settled back into bed to watch some TV on her laptop, only realising how late it was when her eyelids began to droop and she noticed the 'do you want to watch the next episode?' message on the screen. She scrambled out of bed to use the loo before getting some sleep, but as she did, she heard her parents talking while they came up the stairs.

'Trust me, D, it'll work out,' her dad was saying soothingly.

Nova heard her mum sigh. 'But two months is hardly any time. If we don't win this competition and then they go ahead with the rate increase . . .'

Nova slipped quickly across the hallway and into the bathroom, frowning. Was there a problem with the restaurant? Nova had heard the businesswomen from her mum's group talking about rising business rates. Could Eats & Beats be under threat somehow? Suddenly, her concerns about Nathan and Sam seemed trivial, and her slightly grudging feeling about having to *work* at one of the biggest festivals of the year went out of the window. She was going to do everything she could to help her family.

'That's not the turning!' Nova insisted urgently, and her brother flipped off the indicator.

'Haha, whoops, my fault,' Otis said, squinting at the maps app on his mobile, which was secured in a holder on the dashboard. Still, Nova didn't *quite* regret agreeing to travel to Summer Fields with Otis in his car – their parents still insisted that grime music was 'all a bit noisy', whereas she and her brother had been enjoying a full-on karaoke-fest to their favourite bangers.

'There!' she called, pointing to the correct exit. They were travelling faster than the cumbersome Eats & Beats truck that their parents were driving to the site, but Nova could still spot them a bit further back as she peered in the wing mirror.

'Can you take your foot off my glove box, please? I just polished this interior, you know,' Otis was saying as he finally turned off the motorway.

'It's comfy,' Nova protested, fiddling with his phone as the last song ended. In the lull, she regarded her brother out of the side of her eye, taking a breath. 'Ots, I was meaning to ask you. Have Mum or Dad said anything to you about having some issues with the restaurant?'

Otis looked at her. 'Why do you think we schlep to all these festivals every summer?' he asked. 'It's the quiet period, you know that.'

'No, but I mean beyond the usual,' Nova said. 'I . . . I overheard them talking, and—'

'Sis. It's OK. We've had tough times before. Don't worry about it,' he said, though something in his face as she watched him in profile made Nova think her brother had more of a sense of the problems her family might be facing than he was letting on. 'This summer is when you should be kicking back, trust,' he continued. 'Once A levels and uni hit, you won't have this same kind of freedom.' He reached for his phone and put on another playlist. 'Enjoy it!'

Nova grudgingly sat back, returning her foot to his glove box. She'd let it go for now, but she planned to get to the bottom of what was going on.

Her mood picked up as they saw the signs for

Summer Fields, and the tall, waving flags that led up to its iconic main stage on a hill, visible even from the drive in to the site. Nova definitely loved London, but it was amazing to see the rolling green fields and wide-open sky, even if it was a slightly ominous grey at the moment. Despite the fact that they were arriving a full day before the normal punters would be on site, it took a little while to be directed towards the caterers' camping area by the cheery festival staff in high-visibility vests (after the usual slight panic about locating the festival pass they'd been sent). But soon enough, Otis had parked up and was inspecting the mud already accumulating on his tyres and the bottom of his car's paintwork with a dismayed expression while Nova chuckled.

Half an hour or so later, the Eats & Beats truck had pulled up in the plot they'd been allocated, and Nova's dad texted to let them know they'd arrived. Otis decided that it was revenge time on Nova – she was left to put up the tents in the caterers' camping area while he went over there to give their mum and dad a hand with the supplies and set up. Even though the process was super-familiar to her by now, Nova still found herself growling at the tent poles as they refused to comply.

She decided to take a break after getting the three tents set up and before setting about the next task of pumping up the air mattresses. She'd begged her dad to splash out on a motorised pump, but he insisted the foot pump was 'good exercise'. The clouds that had threatened earlier were breaking up, casting a beautiful glow of sunshine over the festival site. Digging in her rucksack, Nova sat down on a log and located the Dictaphone again. She sang a few lines into it, inspired by the fresh air and the break in nature, then smiled, realising that this new tune might actually marry the two things she was really passionate about – her songwriting and her love of the environment. She was already pleased to see so many water stations around the site for refilling bottles, and the festival organisers had made a pledge about reducing plastic wherever possible. She didn't want to get too high and mighty about it, but as she added a few more lines to the new song she'd been working on, she was pleased that she'd come up with *two* ideas for tunes in as many days. The Dictaphone really did help. For a start, she wasn't distracted by checking for messages from a certain someone when she used it . . .

She sang a few more lines, until she heard someone call over to her.

'That was beautiful, young lady!'

Pauline, one of the other festival regulars who ran a really tasty hot dog stall, was waving at Nova as she walked past, carrying her tent in its case. Nova immediately blushed hotly, realising she'd been singing loud enough for people around her to hear!

'Th-thanks, Pauline,' she managed, quickly putting the Dictaphone away again with a sigh. She was definitely going to have to focus on her environmental passions rather than her own music, if just being overheard like that was giving her the sweats!

Nova turned her attention back to pumping up the mattresses vigorously, and by the time she'd finished, she was sweating for a different reason – but she was triumphant that their beds were all ready.

The festival site was only just starting to bustle with people in the warm afternoon sunshine. Nova couldn't help a quick check of Sam's Instagram feed on her phone as she walked over to the catering area. As there was no indication that he was heading to Summer Fields, she decided to throw herself wholeheartedly into the weird and wonderful things the festival would have to offer, and leave all of that to one side while she was there. Whenever she had time, that was. She'd even spotted a sign for goat yoga, which sounded deeply odd, and hilarious. Maybe she'd try it out!

Arriving at the food trucks, Nova headed around to the back of Eats & Beats and poked her head in. 'How's everything going?' she enquired, and her mum turned around from where she was prepping some vegetables for the next day.

'Oh, fine, darl, all ready to go, I reckon.'

'Cool. Well, the tents are set up, so you should all be extremely grateful!' Nova said with a chuckle. 'Sweated buckets being left to do that!'

'I can tell,' Deana said with a grin, gesturing at her daughter from top to toe: Nova had piled her locs into an unruly bun, over her damp-armpitted T-shirt, and her dusty legs ended in muddy-booted feet.

Nova ambled back out of the truck. She heard a message come through on her phone and pulled it out of her pocket to see Gemma's name. Her text contained several siren emojis, and the words Look at his Insta!!!

Nova was confused, but she obviously knew who her friend was referring to by 'him'.

Sam Rodriguez.

What did Gem mean? Opening the app, Nova stared down at the screen.

Wait, he's just posted something. Are those the Summer Fields flags? Nova thought, looking at the latest post on Sam's page. *Oh God.*

'Nova!' a boy's voice called. It definitely wasn't her brother, or her dad. She looked up and saw who it was coming from.

'Sam . . .' she breathed.

CHAPTER 13

Nova felt a wave of elation sweep over her as she spotted Sam waving and ambling towards her with his long stride.

Ohmygod!

He looked as gorgeous as she remembered – maybe even more so – in his faded jeans and what seemed to be a vintage Prince T-shirt. He pushed his hair back from his forehead, smiling a bit warily at Nova now as he got closer. Just as he reached her, Nova suddenly remembered her post-tent-setup state.

Extra sweaty. Crazy hair. Stinkiness. *Oh. No.*

Sam was now standing right in front of her, and seemed to be opening his arms for a spontaneous hug in greeting. Nova leapt back out of his range, then stumbled on a divot in the grass and had to flail to right herself.

'S-sorry,' she stammered, clamping her arms back down to her sides so he couldn't see the damp patches under them. 'Um, hi. I didn't know you would be here. I mean, I didn't expect . . . I mean, it's really amazing to see you.' *Too strong?* 'Err, I mean good.' *Wow.* She wasn't sure this reunion could be going any worse!

Sam tilted his head to one side a bit, and gave Nova a quizzical look. 'Is it?' he asked, and she was taken all over again by the warm depth of his voice, his accent . . . 'Because the way you hightailed it away from me last time I saw you seemed to suggest it might be otherwise.'

He folded his arms, and Nova felt a cold, metaphorical dash of water dampen her excitement. She scuffed a foot across the ground, looking down to avoid his scrutiny for another reason than her appearance. He genuinely seemed hurt, and she hated that it was her fault.

'Sorry about that,' she said, then risked a glance up at him. His green eyes squinted in the sunshine. 'I mean, I did have to go. But . . . I shouldn't have rushed off like that.'

'Usain Bolt couldn't have moved faster,' he replied, prompting a frown from Nova.

She couldn't help feeling a bit confused. If Sam was really annoyed with her, why was he there talking to her at all? She looked at him fully now, feeling bolder as that sensible part of her brain took over, telling her not to get too excited at Sam showing up again. Did he just want to make her feel bad?

'Well, if you wanted to, you could have . . . I don't know, found my socials? Or even stopped by – we were still packing up the next morning,' she said.

Sam sighed, releasing his crossed arms. His softened stance seemed reflected in his eyes and Nova tried not to melt. 'I tried,' he told her. 'I did want to come see you. But my dad was all about taking off.' He paused, looking down for a moment. 'Anyway, we left real early that morning, and . . . Honestly, I was kind of bummed out at the way our date ended. I figured I'd put myself on the line enough already, so I wanted to give you a little space.' He drew in a breath, and Nova really did feel bad all over again. Though she felt a bit better as a small quirk found Sam's lips. 'I mean, you couldn't have looked *me* up, though? Come on, I told that whole crowd at the open mic my Insta handle just for your benefit . . .'

Nova felt herself heat up again even as a smile formed on her face. 'I might have checked it out,' she said.

'Oh yeah?' He bent down a little to catch her eye again. 'Didn't want to throw me a "like" or . . .'

Nova felt embarrassment creep up from the soles of her feet as she laughed. 'When I see something worthy of one, I will.'

Sam clutched his broad chest, screwing up his face. 'Ouch. Oh wow.'

'I'm joking . . .'

'Nah, I'm gonna make it my mission to do something worthy of your approval, Ms Clarke,' he said, then took a step closer. 'I was going to pretend like I just stumbled by the truck here, but truth is I've been wandering around all the different food areas for, like, an hour trying to find it, since I knew you'd be around here somewhere. And let me tell you, this festival is *insanely* huge,' he said with a self-deprecating chuckle.

He . . . was looking for me?

'Thanks for coming to find me,' Nova said, her throat feeling dry.

'You're not going to run away again, are you?' he asked, his voice a mixture of humour and genuine concern.

Staring up at him, Nova suddenly remembered again the state she was in, and cleared her throat. 'Um, no, it's just . . . I should go and sort myself out – I've been setting up our tents so I'm just feeling a bit icky,' she told him. He raised an eyebrow, and she crossed her heart. 'Honest!'

'Well, to be safe, I'm going to grab your number this time,' Sam said, reaching around to his back pocket to pull out his phone. Nova was jealous – it was the latest model. Gemma had mentioned that she was planning to guilt her dad into getting her one in the airport on their way to Mexico, which was the day it was coming out, so somehow Sam was ahead of the curve. Apparently, Gem thought the better-quality camera would be good for her online book reviews.

Sam began to hand the phone over to her, then pulled back so he could unlock it first, but not before Nova took a glance at it.

'Is that your mum?' she asked. The picture on the home screen had been of a beautiful woman with long, dark hair. She had one hand on the shoulder of a grinning little boy. He handed the phone back to Nova.

As she typed in her number, he told her, 'Yeah, that's my ma, and my little brother, Teo.'

'And they're back in Miami?' she asked, returning the phone. He smiled down at the screen.

'Yeah.' She heard her own mobile ringing, and looked at it to see an unfamiliar number appear on the screen.

'Just checking,' Sam said with a grin. 'Don't want you giving me the number of your favourite take-out or something . . .'

Nova put one hand on her hip. 'Give me some credit! Plus, who doesn't order via app these days?'

Sam pocketed his phone again, his face settling again into a slightly more contemplative expression. 'I do miss them. My mom really had to deal with a lot, you know, being a single parent. And before that . . .' He shook his head, pushing his hair off his face again. 'That's a story for another time,' he said, his brows knitting for a moment, but then smiling. 'You've got somewhere to be and all.'

Nova had almost forgotten. 'Yeah. Um, maybe we can meet up later or something? I mean, I'll be pretty busy with the truck while we're here, but—'

'We'll find time, Nova Clarke.' Sam reached

over and lifted a stray loc away from her face while she stared dumbly at him. Sam's lips quirked again and, with a little salute, he turned to amble away.

'I actually asked to make sure it wasn't too spicy?' a woman with a pinched mouth, short, wispy brown hair and a child who was merrily dousing the side of the food truck with a bottle of the hot sauce usually left on the serving counter was saying the next day.

Nova didn't even have to grit her teeth as she gave the woman a semi-apologetic smile – that was how good a mood she was in! 'Sorry about that. I did suggest maybe the curry chicken wasn't the best option . . .'

The kid was happily stuffing the food in his mouth. Nova had the feeling he liked it just fine. He managed to distract his mum enough for her to give up on her pointless complaints, and Nova called out an apology to the handful of people in the queue, which was dwindling at long last. Lunchtime had been completely manic, and most of the afternoon had been busy, too. But even Otis' ribbing after hearing about Nova having tried out the goat yoga that morning didn't rattle her.

Sam Rodriguez had actually *come and found her* yesterday, and been his ridiculously charming, gorgeous self. She wasn't sure how she could be expected to ignore that! Still, she was planning on doing what she could to remain cool and composed and not get too gassed over him, just in case. It was tough, because he'd been sending little messages to her all through the day – pictures of him pulling silly faces, including one wearing a very suspect hat made out of balloons. And also sending jokes about their date from the last festival, and clips of the stages he was watching . . . Nova had found herself giggling distractedly at the messages more than once, to the raised eyebrow of her mum.

She pulled out her phone eagerly now as another

alert came through, but this time it wasn't from Sam – it was a reminder Nova had set herself.

'Oh, Mum, it's four-fifteen. Am I OK to head to Deliah's talk?' She had been beside herself when she had seen that Delilah Adeyemi was speaking at the festival. The Nigerian woman was one of Nova's idols – a real pioneer of environmental science, who was also ridiculously cool. Nova had spent hours watching videos of her talks and following her on social media, where she interspersed her campaigning with Beyoncé references and epic clap-backs to idiots who tried to deny climate change.

'Of course, sweetheart,' her mum said, and Nova eagerly untied her apron, hanging it by the door.

'I'll be back by six-thirty for the evening rush,' she called. As she pulled up the map of the festival site to figure out where she should be going, Nova saw another message from Sam. She opened it to reveal a picture of him eating a patty, standing outside a truck gaudily branded with a huge Jamaican flag. He was pulling a face and giving it a thumbs-down, with the caption: Note to self never to deviate from Eats & Beats, even if it is so I avoid looking like a stalker. She laughed at her screen, then closed his message, impulsively screen-shotting the site map. She added a circle around The Meadow, the area where she was going to hear Delilah speak, and added it to a message to Sam.

Challenge – meet me by the statue made of recycling here in 5 mins. If the site's not too insanely huge . . . ☺

As she hit *send*, Nova wondered if letting him in on just how passionate she was about Delilah and her environmental campaigning was a bit too personal, but she'd done it now. She also wondered if she stank of cooking again! She was definitely not on a Gemma-approved level of date-ready, but this wasn't a date, was it? Her army-fatigue style trousers and white vest top had a 90s feel that she was into. Either way, it would have to do!

She navigated her way through the huge crowds to the quieter area near The Meadow, and located the statue she'd mentioned to Sam. Adjusting and readjusting her loose locs around her shoulders, Nova tried to seem nonchalant, feeling a bit more sympathy for how Sam must have felt when he was waiting for her that night at Island Rocks.

A few minutes later, she was about to give up when she heard the whir of one of the electric golf buggies staff and performers used to be ferried around the site as it pulled up nearby. To her surprise, Sam jumped out of it, waving eagerly. His dad being a roadie clearly had its perks! The driver in the high-vis vest waved at Sam as he pulled away again. Nova gave him a broad smile, before mock-frowning and tapping her imaginary watch.

'Am I late?' he asked breathlessly, jogging over to her.

Nova relented and shook her head. 'No, you made it. And you're in for a treat!' She led the way towards a low stage encircled by trees, whose leaves left dappled sunlight on the ground where eager people were gathering, sitting cross-legged on the ground, waiting for Delilah to take the stage. Nova picked her way to the front and sat down directly in the path of the mic so they could get the best view. Sam folded his tall frame down next to Nova, and she let out an unrestrained 'whoop' as a beautiful black woman with hip-length box braids and a bright green dress strode out, waving, to a huge swell of applause.

'Simmer down, Ms Clarke!' Sam said, nudging her teasingly. Nova felt a spark of electricity at the warmth of his touch against her arm, and took a breath before focussing all her attention back towards the stage. She hung on Delilah's every word for the forty-five-minute talk, and when the speaker finally finished up with a joke, burst into a standing ovation as she left the stage.

'Ah-mazing!' Nova said, turning to Sam.

He laughed, and then his expression softened as he stared at Nova. She looked away bashfully, and he took a breath. 'She was great, you're right. So you weren't kidding about being into this environment stuff, huh? That lady was, like, your Harry Styles or something! The shrieking!' He pretended to massage his ears. It was Nova's turn to nudge him now, and he rocked back a bit, playfully, then righted himself by folding his tanned arms around his bent knees.

'She's just really inspiring,' Nova said earnestly. 'I feel like a lot of what she was saying I could apply to our restaurant. I might even see if I can get something going at school . . . She's really about making a difference, you know? Not like celebs just giving lip service to it. I mean, I saw that Flightpath guy getting a private jet the other day, when he's always banging on about the environment. Practise what you preach, I reckon! Like, it's a bit hypocritical to . . .' She tailed off as Sam's expression made her think *she'd* been banging on about it a bit too much, but after a moment he smiled.

'What, so you're never getting in an airplane?' he asked. His eyes twinkled mischievously. 'Say,

Solange, Frank Ocean, Billie Eilish and Lizzo are all playing a once-in-a-lifetime concert in New York, you're not flying over there?'

Nova bit the inside of her cheek. 'Well, there's carbon offsetting. And there are other modes of transport, you know . . . But OK, fine. Throw in Esperanza Spalding and I'm there,' she finished with a grin.

He laughed. 'You know, I wasn't kidding before, Nova. It's really cool to see you so passionate about this,' he told her, holding eye contact again. Nova checked her phone to distract herself, and saw the time.

'OK, it's not a lie, but I do need to be getting back to the truck again soon. Sorry. It's kind of going to be the story of my life for now. I need to be around to help out a bit more at the minute,' Nova explained, fiddling with the hem of her top as she spoke. 'I think my mum and dad could use a bit more support for the business.'

Sam waited until she looked up again, then softly said, 'It's cool, Nova. Your parents seem pretty dope. It's great you guys are all getting to spend time together as a family, even if it is crazy busy.' Something in his eyes told her that he understood slightly tougher things than his happy-go-lucky exterior would suggest. Nova thought back to the picture of his family on his phone.

'Missing your mum and brother, yeah?' He nodded. 'I suppose it's nice your dad wanted to spend some one-on-one time with you, though?'

Sam shrugged. He didn't seem too convinced. 'I guess. Not that there's a whole lot of that going on. He has a new girlfriend or whatever . . .'

Nova nodded sympathetically. 'Gemma's going through some parental issues, too,' she said. 'Remember, my best mate—?'

'The reason we're here together right now? She of the inflatable chair? How could I forget?' he said, aiming another of his devastating grins Nova's way. He stood up and offered her a hand, and as she grasped it, Nova got flashbacks of the electricity she'd felt with him on their Island Rocks date.

'Let's get you back to that truck . . .'

As they headed out of The Meadow area, one of the guys who had helped put on the talk asked if they'd be up for signing a petition to lobby parliament about stricter emission guidelines.

'Like you could hold this one back,' Sam quipped, nodding towards Nova, but he took the pen first with a comical flourish. He began to write, but then he scribbled out his name, frowning suddenly. 'Whoops. I mean, sorry. Uh, for a second there I forgot I'm from the other side of the pond. I guess I can use my dad's address . . .' He started again.

Nova signed too, and then felt a thrill as Sam took her hand once more. They wandered back towards Eats & Beats, passing one of the bigger stages. A massive placard had been set up nearby with the running times of the performers due to play there, and they paused beside it as Nova shook her head.

'It's mad that there are basically all men on the line-up here, when there are so many incredible female artists making the most amazing music.'

Sam nodded. 'It is pretty lame,' he said, then turned to her with a sly look on his face. 'But I think I know a way you could change that.'

Nova felt immediately wary. 'Oh yeah?'

'The chick from the open mic I did at Island Rocks hit me up. They have an acoustic performance space set up here, too. I was thinking of checking it out tomorrow night. But there I go, another *man* potentially on the bill . . . Know any amazing, beautiful, talented female singer-songwriters from London who might be willing to give it a shot?'

Nova sighed. 'Subtle,' she said, and he smiled. 'I just . . . I write for me, Sam. I'm not really ready to share it yet. Who knows if I'll ever be?'

He turned to face her, using one finger to lift her chin. 'Well, the only real way to know if you're ready is to just go for it, right?' he said, his voice low. He didn't move his hand, but instead inched closer to her. Nova's heart began to race, and she swallowed hard as he licked his lips.

He's going to kiss me. Wow, he's really about to kiss me . . .

But just then, a huge flash of light in the darkening sky above them made Nova jump. It was followed by a deafening clap of thunder. Sam's hand dropped away. Seconds later, Nova felt fat drops of warm rain on her face, falling slowly at first – and then a deluge began to dump down on them. She and Sam both burst into laughter, and he grabbed her hand again. Together they ran towards the food trucks, giggling. But Nova's *mind* was racing, too. And her lips were electric with the possibility of a kiss to come.

CHAPTER 14

The next morning, Nova scrunched up her face as she felt something wet splash on it. Was she dreaming about yesterday afternoon? But in fact, she realised, her whole pillow felt damp. The air definitely didn't feel warm enough for it to be sweat – plus, that would have been rank – but as she reluctantly opened her eyes, another splash hit her dead between the eyes. Then she noticed the unmistakable sound of rain pattering hard on to the top of her tent. And clearly, it was coming in through the seams, too.

Fantastic!

After pulling her fold-up cagoule out of its pouch and putting it on, Nova unzipped her tent and was faced with an early morning deluge. Overnight, the stormy showers that had forced her and Sam to run for cover before (regretfully) having to say goodbye and get back to work, had turned full-on and unrelenting. The ground was brown and squidgy with churned-up earth. Nova looked up to see her mum's bizarrely cheerful face emerge from her tent as she zipped up her wax jacket.

'Wellies time, Nov! Wouldn't be Summer Fields without a bit of mud, right?'

Wellies. Nova's heart sank. How could she have possibly been so stupid? Maybe because the weather up until now had been so good, she'd completely forgotten her old reliable green wellies, which were currently standing to attention by the front door back at their flat.

Great.

Regretfully, Nova pulled on her trainers and grabbed her wash bag to at least brush her teeth

– a shower seemed a bit pointless given that mud splashed up her legs with every step.

By the time she trudged back to her tent, the rain was easing a bit, but her shoes were dirty, sticky and damp. Could this day get any worse? Apparently so – Otis was rummaging in the back of his car for something with a frown on his face.

'What's up?' Nova called over to him, and he straightened.

'Trying to find my Phillips head screwdriver – it must have fallen out of my tool kit. The truck's generator's packed up . . .'

Nova's heart sank. If they couldn't fix it themselves, that would surely be an expensive thing to repair. 'Is there anything I can do to help?' she asked.

'Ah, here we go!' Otis said, then shut the car and turned to her with a reassuring smile. 'Nah, no worries. Tony from Who Ate All the Pies is giving me a hand, we should get it sorted in a couple of hours. Hey, at least you'll get a bit of time to yourself.' He glanced down at her trainers with a smirk and shook his head. 'Ooh, unlucky, Nov. Those creps are *done*.'

Nova pursed her lips. 'Yeah, you don't say.' But she was glad that it sounded like her brother was taking control – he was always good at practical stuff, fixing things. No wonder he wanted to study engineering at uni. Maybe this *was* a good chance to relax a bit. She sent a message to the family group chat to check her parents didn't need her, and then checked the balance on her account. She wasn't exactly rolling in it, but given the state of the ground, Nova decided it was probably worth shelling out for some new wellies – they were going to be here for a few days yet, and she didn't fancy getting foot rot! And Nova had to admit the free time did have one major positive – she might actually have some time to hang out with Sam. He'd sent her a quick goodnight text the previous night. She opened up his last message and hit reply.

¡Buenos dias! (Impressed?! Lol). This weather is nasty! I'm expecting Noah to turn up in an ark any moment. But on the plus side I have the morning off & I'm going out in search of wellies. Where are you camped, shall I come and find you after?

She set out into the festival site as she waited for Sam to reply, but after five minutes he still hadn't responded. She tried not to get antsy about it – maybe he was having a lie in. Instead, she made her way towards the huge array of stalls selling more wares than Nova could imagine would possibly be needed at a festival. Gemma would have been in heaven! But even though it was early, Nova noticed something with a sinking feeling that wasn't just caused by the mud. Wellington boots were almost all sold out everywhere. She found one decent pair, but they were three sizes too big. The only pair that she located that weren't extortionately priced or completely the wrong fit were iridescent, and covered with cringe-worthy emoji symbols. Still, fashion would have to go out of the window since the clouds were definitely beginning to gather again overhead. Reluctantly, Nova tapped her card to pay at the stall's till and then took off her trainers and pulled on the boots, stuffing her mud-logged shoes into a paper bag.

But speaking of emojis . . . Nova pulled out her phone again eagerly – and to her relief, a message from Sam was waiting for her.

Morning off, you say? Darn, and I'm just waking up now! Gimme 10, I'll come find you at the truck if that's cool?

Nova smiled, and replied quickly that it was fine. It might be a good idea to go and check on how things were going with the generator anyway. She started making her way over towards the food trucks. Her new boots made her progress less squelchy, but after a few minutes, she realised that she'd been so distracted by thinking about Sam she'd been walking in the wrong direction.

Turning, Nova came to some wooden planks which formed a series of walkways over to what she realised was the VIP area – mainly because of the number of people in expensive oversized parkas laughing loudly, the culturally inappropriate and no-doubt ludicrously pricey headdresses being worn despite the rain, and the kids whose parents probably gave them £200 passes to the festival as stocking-fillers last Christmas. Not that Nova was bitter or anything!

Rolling her eyes, she turned to head back in the other direction . . . and slammed straight into a tall, redheaded woman who was barking orders into a phone. Nova tripped over part of the wooden walkway as they collided, and fell straight into a muddy puddle. The woman stepped over her, glaring at Nova as though she was the one who was inconvenienced!

'Yes. She should be here in twenty,' the woman was saying loudly on her call. 'Yes, they're choppering her in now . . . *Yes* . . . That's what I just said! I can practically hear the rotor blades now, and where are you? Nowhere to be seen! She'll need a make-up touch-up . . .' The self-important woman was bellowing now, plugging her ear with one manicured finger and striding away without a second glance at Nova.

'Nah, don't mind me!' Nova muttered, along with a few other choice words under her breath as she struggled to stand. But then a shadow fell over her and she looked up. 'Err, Sam? Wh-what are you doing here?'

He was leaning down, a mixture of concern and bemusement on his handsome face as he quickly helped Nova up. 'I was just, uh, heading across the site to meet you.' His arm remained around her as he asked, 'Jeez, are you OK?'

'Yeah, just muddy,' she said, but she felt the tension in her muscles relax a little as Sam rubbed, seemingly unconsciously, between her shoulder blades. Even through her rain cagoule, she could feel the tingling heat of his warm hand. 'Thanks,' she said breathily. 'Good thing you were passing by!'

'Yeah,' he said, releasing her at last and assessing her from the ground up. 'Interesting boots,' he added with a smile, but it faded as Nova flicked a bit of churned-up grass from her hand at him. His eyes sparked at her challenge, and she pretended to cower in anticipation of potential retaliation.

'These boots are the least of my problems now I'm totally covered in mud,' she told him with a sigh, wiping her hands on her sodden denim shorts and feeling the dampness seeping through her thin jacket into her T-shirt. Sam nodded sympathetically.

'You're right.' He moved them towards the thick canvas that sectioned off the nearby VIP area. Edging the fabric aside with a foot, he held it open and nodded at Nova. 'But I have a feeling this place will have plenty of stuff you could use to clean up? I, uh, I heard there's a massage parlour and a manicurist in there, all kinds of crazy stuff . . . !'

Nova was tempted, but shot him an unsure look.

189

'OK, *mira*. No need for the wide eyes, cute as they are. I have an in here – my dad knows the security guys, so they won't give us any trouble,' he said with a chuckle. Nova batted him playfully on the shoulder, relieved. 'Come on!'

Sam led the way around to the entrance, and nodded wordlessly at a huge bald guy with an earpiece who was standing guard.

'Who would've thought that being a roadie's son would come with actual decent perks?' Nova said with a giggle. 'I'm beginning to regret only ever hanging out with the catering people!'

Sam shrugged as he smiled back at her. Nova's eyes felt like they were on stalks as they moved into the exclusive enclosure. This wasn't just the area for people who'd shelled out a bit more money for access to decent showers. Sam was right – there was all sorts of pampering stuff set up, with bored-looking attendants sitting at each station, surrounded by more celeb-hanger-on types. Everywhere was clean and wooden and smelled of scented candles and luxury. They even had a DJ spinning mellow tunes on actual *vinyl*. Nova found herself singing along to a weird remix of a Stevie Wonder tune, ignoring Sam's wide, appreciative grin as she harmonised a few lines, then cutting off to exclaim, 'Ooh, loos!' as they passed a wide door from which two fragrant brunettes dressed head to toe in white (*white!*) fluttering outfits emerged. 'I'm going to clean up a bit in here if that's OK?'

'Cool. How 'bout I see what I can rustle up for you to change into?' Sam said. Nova raised an eyebrow dubiously and he laughed. 'Trust me. See you back here in a minute.'

Nova was very tempted to get into the inviting-looking full shower that was in one section of the bathroom, but she settled for stripping off her jacket and washing her arms and legs off in the sink, smiling at the rolls of white fluffy towels stacked up nearby. She grabbed one and was drying off with it when a girl who couldn't have been more than twelve emerged from one of the cubicles and shot her a judgemental look that almost made Nova laugh out loud. She was thrilled to be feeling a bit less gross, though, and she pulled some lip gloss from her bag, swiping it on in a vague attempt to look a bit more alluring before she headed back out.

Sam was leaning against the wall outside the bathroom, and when she opened the door he held a T-shirt out to her with a wide grin. 'Thought you were such a big fan, you'd appreciate this,' he said. The top was emblazoned with the cover of Flightpath's latest album. The band had been a last-minute addition as headliners on the bill at Summer Fields when the original act had to drop out.

'Seriously?' Nova asked, though she was smiling too.

'Would you rather be damp? It's free!'

Nova folded her arms, trying to cover her amused smirk as she stared at him, then reached out and grabbed the T-shirt from Sam's hands. 'OK, fine,' she told him, turning on her heel and returning to the bathroom to the sound of his chuckle. She went into one of the cubicles to put the top on, balling up her damp blue tee and putting it into her backpack. Nova came out of the stall and was rearranging her locs in the mirror when she realised another woman was in the bathroom with her. Nova locked eyes with the woman in the reflection as she washed her hands, and had to stop herself from fan-girling. The woman had unmistakeable black snake tattoos encircling her slender arms, and her white vest top was stark against her light brown skin. It was *Pia Jones*, an up-and-coming alt-R'n'B singer who Nova absolutely loved.

And . . . her eyes had just settled on to Nova's brand new Flightpath T-shirt!

'Hey,' the woman said with an almost pitying smile, while Nova tried to formulate words to deny any allegiance to this tragically uncool band. But before she could speak, Pia had dried her hands and left the bathroom again.

Mortifying!

CHAPTER 15

Nova shook her head as she returned to where Sam was standing outside the bathroom.

'You have no idea how much I've already been humiliated by this top,' she said wryly, emphatically doing up her jacket over the T-shirt. 'That was only one of my favourite new artists, who now thinks I'm eagerly putting my lighter in the air to chart hits!'

Sam laughed long and loud, but Nova was distracted from his mirth as he threw a consoling arm over her shoulder and steered her away towards a bar area.

'Aww,' he said, but Nova detected sarcasm. She didn't mind, though, as he squeezed her closer to him. 'Why don't we get you one of these fruity concoctions and a canapé or two to help you get over it!'

He wasn't wrong – the drinks were delicious, a non-alcoholic punch that gave Nova some ideas for a new beverage to add to the Eats & Beats menu. And the snacks were incredible, too.

'Is that actual *lobster*?' Nova asked, looking at little bowls of finger foods with her mouth watering. 'Why would you ever go anywhere else to eat?'

Sam handed her one of the bowls and took one of his own. He seemed amused, but cast a slightly disparaging look at their surroundings. 'Are you kidding? Look at this place,' he said. 'These over-privileged VIP types only care about being seen by other vacant-lot types like themselves. It's too fake.'

He kind of had a point – Nova had not missed the judgemental glances she had been cast,

195

seemingly assessing and then dismissing her when they realised she wasn't 'someone'.

'Yeah, I get what you mean.' She shot him a wry look. 'Then again, you do live in Miami. Isn't that full of plastic people, too?'

Sam smiled around a skewer of chargrilled chicken, chewing and swallowing. 'Well, depends where you hang out and who you hang out with. But sure, there's plenty of fakery back home, too. Especially if . . . Well, you know, people are always interested in making a buck, or being around whoever might give them shine. I mostly stick to a few buddies, and my family of course.'

Nova leaned against a nearby tall table, cocking her head to one side to assess Sam as she sipped on her drink. 'Tell me more about them,' she said. 'Your family, I mean.'

The light that came into Sam's face at that suggestion made Nova smile. She understood that immediate feeling of affection.

'My mom is, like, one of the most selfless people I know. She runs an afterschool programme for black and Latinx kids in our neighbourhood, even though if she wanted to she could just chill, you know? I mean, uh, we do all right, in terms of my dad and alimony or whatever.'

Nova tried not to show surprise that Sam's dad was decently well off. Maybe roadies got paid more than she'd assumed. 'She sounds really cool,' she said, and he nodded, a smile spreading on his face.

'And my little bro Teo is awesome, too. I mean, the boy is a handful! He's lucky, though. He's had a little more time to just be a kid, whereas I . . .' Sam's face grew more serious. 'I guess I felt like I had to look out for him as his big brother. Protect him, you know, from some of the stuff with our parents. Our dad, specifically . . .'

Nova edged a little closer to Sam, looking up at him with concern. She asked softly, 'Were things . . . difficult at home?' She wanted to be sensitive about it. Nova knew she was lucky, and very grateful that her parents were still so solid and in love, and supported one another. She couldn't imagine how hard it would be to go through your mum and dad splitting up.

'Yeah,' Sam answered. 'You could say that.' He sighed. 'My dad drank a whole lot, and so . . . It was tough. I mean, he's doing way better now, but . . .'

'But that must still be really hard to have had to deal with,' Nova said quietly, reaching over to place her hand over Sam's where it rested on the table between them. Their eyes connected, and she saw the emotions swimming in his – and no doubt in her own.

Just then, there was a ripple of whispers and excitement, and she looked over towards an area sectioned off with white beaded curtains. The rude red-headed woman from earlier was now ushering a tall, willowy model-type through the VIP area, towards where she and Sam were partaking of the food and drink. Nova felt Sam's hand at her elbow unexpectedly, and he quickly steered her away towards some gigantic bean bags. He pulled her down on to one, kicking the other bags aside as if to shield them from view. Nova wasn't sure if her surprise was more from the sudden proximity of being smushed on to a bean bag with Sam, or the urgency with which he'd moved her away from the bar.

'Sorry, my bad,' he said. Nova had a chance to study his gorgeous face up close as his eyes darted over her shoulder, back towards where they had been standing. 'Uh, I thought I saw one of the other stewards who has a bit more of a stick up his butt about unauthorised participation . . .' He finally looked back at her, and seemed to realise himself how close together they were – close enough that Nova could see the little flecks of gold in his deep green eyes, and the freckles in his darkly tanned skin.

They both jumped at the sound of a loud voice behind them. 'OK, so Sadie, we'll get you set up here with hair and make-up in just a minute, and then they'll get started with the shoot . . .' It was the red-headed woman again, and now Nova realised that she had been ushering Sadie Varma in to the VIP area. Why was it always her, ruining things? Sam still seemed on edge as he heard the woman speaking. He sprang back up from the bean bag, pulling Nova with him.

'You know what, I've actually just realised it's getting towards time for that open mic I was telling you about. I left my guitar out front before I found you. Let's go pick it up, and head over there?' Sam said, heading swiftly back towards where they had first come in, tugging Nova along by the hand. When they got to the entrance, he gestured to something behind the steward with an apologetic smile, and the guy turned around and grabbed the case that clearly contained Sam's guitar.

'Let me fetch you an umbrella too, Mr—'

'Cool, thanks a lot, man!' Sam said, taking the brolly quickly with a smile. They passed a blonde girl handing out promotional tote bags stuffed with eco-friendly toiletries. The girl gave Sam a wide, flirtatious smile, but he grabbed one of the bags and handed it straight over to Nova with a wink. OK, all the rushing around was forgiven!

Sam put up the umbrella, and threw his arm around Nova again as they laughed, huddling under it and trying to fight their way through the rain-soaked crowds towards the acoustic tent.

Finally they found the right place, but it looked like this was a bit more of a formal affair than the last open-mic Nova had seen Sam perform at. There was a chalkboard set up next to the stage, and it already had his name on it.

The same woman who had been running the tent at Island Rocks was introducing someone onstage, and the tent was getting quite full. Lots of people were seated on rugs like before, but there were also a good number of people standing around the edges of the tent, too. Sam took Nova's hand as he made his way closer to the stage and over to a tall, bearded guy standing at the side of it. The man had an earpiece in, and Sam let him know he was there.

'Nice one, mate – you'll be on in ten minutes or so, yeah?' The beardy guy held a dark piece of fabric aside, nodding to them to head in. The space was a makeshift backstage area with a few fold-out chairs and cans of water on a trestle table.

'Coming up in the world, eh?' Nova said, impressed in spite of herself.

'Oh yeah, this is the big time!' Sam said ironically, gesturing around them.

Nova popped open a can of water. 'No, seriously, Sam – this is really cool. That audience is pretty big, though. Are you nervous?'

He had pulled his guitar out of its case and was holding it closer to his ear while he tuned it. He glanced at Nova and shrugged. 'Not really.'

'*How*?' she enquired, heading back to peek out at the gathering crowd and the lights trained towards the stage. 'I would be *bricking* it, especially if I was going to perform my own stuff.' She practically *was* bricking it, and it wasn't even her who was about to play! She turned back to Sam, who was regarding her with an expression that for some reason made her almost blush.

'I focus in on one thing,' he said, his voice low. 'One person, sometimes . . . and imagine I'm just playing to them.' He held her gaze, putting his guitar down and moving closer, but they sprang apart as the bearded guy stepped into the space, ushering in another performer – a girl with a blunt bob carrying a flute – backstage. Out at the front, a round of applause indicated that the first act was finishing up.

'Err, Sam, isn't it? You're up next, mate,' the burly man said to him, nodding once at Nova before he disappeared again. On the stage, Nova could hear the woman hyping up the crowd, describing how incredible Sam's performance had been at Island Rocks.

'. . . so please welcome back to our stage, the rising star, Sam Rodriguez!'

Sam picked up his guitar and walked towards the curtain, and without thinking, Nova stood up on tiptoes to kiss his cheek as he passed. He flushed as he pushed the curtain aside and bounded up on to the stage. Quickly, Nova edged out to stand at the side of the stage so that she could watch Sam perform.

'Hey, how you doing?' he asked the crowd, and Nova scanned their reaction. The girls in particular seemed suddenly very attentive, unsurprisingly, but Sam turned to his side and spotted Nova standing down at the side of the stage. He played a few chords on his guitar, adjusting the microphone, and then took a breath, his face more serious than it had been the last time she saw him play.

'This . . . This is a song about my dad,' he said.

Sam began to play a melancholy melody, and his deep voice was full of emotion as he started to sing, closing his eyes. He seemed to keep them shut almost for the whole performance, playing his heart out. The song's lyrics were about abandonment, fear and anger. Nova was absolutely transfixed as she watched Sam play. He was so incredibly talented, she forgot everything except watching him on the stage. As he finished, he opened his eyes and they were fixed on her again. She burst into whoops and applause, just as the rest of the audience did, and he finally broke into a smile, directed at her and then back out to the crowd.

'*Qué triste*, huh?' He smiled self-deprecatingly. 'Uh, what do you say we liven things up a little?'

His next song was more upbeat, with a clear Cuban influence, and again he added some percussion using the body of his guitar. The audience were absolutely lapping it up. Nova danced at the side of the stage, loving every moment. She hardly realised when Sam segued into a familiar Stevie Wonder tune, and he started speaking on the mic over his guitar strumming.

'OK, now we're cooking! I want to invite a really special friend up here to help me out – I think she's going to kill me, though, so I need you all to make her feel super-welcome. Nova Clarke!'

Nova was still bopping along to his playing, but froze as she heard him say her name.

'Wh-what?'

'Come on – I know you know this one!' Sam was saying, grinning down at her from the stage. Nova shook her head.

'Err, I . . .'

Sam got the crowd clapping in time, and then took a few steps across the stage, leaning down towards her. 'If you really don't want to, I won't force you, beautiful,' he said. 'But I'll be right here. Just focus on me.' The way he was looking at her made Nova feel calm and hot and excited all at the same time. She felt a fizz of energy as Sam reached down towards her, and before Nova knew it, she was slipping her hand into his.

He pulled her on to the stage, and then returned to strumming enthusiastically. He turned the microphone towards her, and she drew in a breath . . .

. . . and began to sing.

Nova heard her voice coming over the speakers and almost stopped, but as she looked over, she saw Sam looking straight at her, grinning from ear to ear encouragingly. She decided to take his advice and pretend she was singing directly to him, which wasn't too hard when he started leaning towards her to add harmonies into the same microphone, his face only inches away from hers. Nova squeezed her eyes shut, giving the finale her absolute all. She was almost shocked as the song finished, still gasping for breath as the crowd burst into rapturous applause. Sam grabbed her hand and held it aloft like a prize fighter. She almost felt like she *had* won something!

'Give it up for Nova Clarke, everybody. Wow!' he shouted, and the crowd whooped. He led her down into a bow, still holding her hand. 'Thank you so much!' Then Sam led Nova off the stage, as the woman who was running the tent bounded over to take the mic again.

'What a duet, am I right, ladies and gents?' Nova heard her saying, but her heart was pounding so loudly in her ears that it almost seemed muffled.

Had she really just done that? Backstage, in the dark area behind the curtains, Sam spun Nova towards him, flipping his guitar on to his back. He pulled her into an embrace, and this time Nova's heart almost felt like it had stopped beating altogether. Sam tightened his arms around her, and she pressed her face into his shoulder. The momentum of his hug made them both shift from side to side, and she felt his voice vibrating through his chest almost as much as she could hear it close to her ear.

'I cannot *believe* how good that was! Like, you were built for this, Nova. You were incredible!'

Nova couldn't speak. The adrenaline was coursing through her veins, and before she knew it, Sam had slackened his embrace enough to look down at her. His eyes were trained on her mouth, and then she saw them close gently as he moved in. He exhaled ever so slightly, his hands warm on her back – and then his lips pressed against hers. Nova closed her eyes too, finding her tiptoes as Sam kissed her, his mouth moving over hers softly.

After what felt like an eternity, he pulled back reluctantly.

'Thank you,' he whispered. Around them, the sounds of the next performer, the crowd, and the festival outside the tent became more noticeable, but Nova tuned them out again, mesmerised by the look on Sam's face as she stared up at him.

'For what?' she asked.

'Trusting me.'

And then he kissed her again.

PART III
WildArts

CHAPTER 16

Nova stared at her phone, a weird mixture of embarrassment, pride and gooey romantic feelings flooding her as she watched the video for the fourth time. *Sam Rodriguez & Nova Clarke – Lumina Tent, Summer Fields*. The video someone had uploaded online had several thousand views already, which she knew was not much in the scheme of things – some of Gemma's book reviews on her channel had more than double that – but it felt so strange and exciting to see a recording of that night online for all the world to see!

The footage was a bit shaky and the audio

quality wasn't amazing, but Nova actually had to admit she sounded pretty good. She and Sam were great singing together. And then remembering that incredible kiss that had happened afterwards . . . She shut her laptop, smiling to herself as she reached for another tissue. Her fingers rooted around and came up empty. She moved her computer aside on her duvet, which was pulled up around her in spite of the summer warmth in the flat. Of course, the minute they got back from Summer Fields, she had to come down with the flu. Who gets the flu in July?

'Ots?' Nova shouted croakily, banging on the wall behind her. She could hear her brother jabbering into his head mic, playing his computer game in the living room. The restaurant was quiet, so their parents had given him the night off. 'Otis!' She went into a coughing fit, regretting raising her voice. She picked up her mobile and hit dial.

'Swear down, are you actually ringing me from within this flat?' came her brother's voice, both on the other end, and also through the wall. She laughed, and then coughed again.

'I've run out of tissues. Come on, do your favourite sis a favour?'

A moment later, Otis appeared at her bedroom door with a fresh box, shaking his head disparagingly even as he tossed them towards her. 'Do you want some more boil soup?' he asked. Her mum had made a hearty pot of the broth for her this morning before she and their dad had started work, and Otis actually offering to get her some was a turn up for the books. Nova smiled.

'Wouldn't say no,' she croaked. Otis rolled his eyes but dutifully headed to the kitchen.

It had been a few days since Summer Fields had ended. Nova had felt like she was floating on air the whole rest of the time they had been there, even when she was working at the truck, and even after getting back and being struck down by this lurgy. She felt another broad smile cross her face as her phone screen illuminated with a message – an Instagram DM. She had a feeling she knew why it was coming through.

Whoa. Are you kidding? I've done it!? I've got an actual, honest to goodness LIKE from the great Nova Clarke? I mean, a little narcissistic that you're in that clip too, but I'll take it . . .

Nova laughed. Sam had added part of the video she had been watching to his feed, and she'd decided he deserved a little acknowledgment for captioning it 'The Most . . . The Most Everything. Nova Clarke' and a heart. She messaged Sam back now with a shrugging emoji and a face blowing a kiss, still feeling a frisson of hope and excitement – and the tiniest bit of trepidation – in doing so.

I miss you, Nova, he sent back, and she wished all over again that Sam wasn't in Madrid with his dad. Something about a tour his father must have been working on. Sam had felt obliged to go with him, since the whole point of being over in the UK was to spend more time with him. Not that Sam being in *London* would have made much difference right now, since Nova was trapped under her duvet with the shivers and sweats.

216

'Who've you been mooning at, anyway?' her brother said, appearing again while carrying a tray of the steaming soup. 'It's messing with my equilibrium seeing you grinning twenty-four/seven.' Nova quickly put her phone down.

'Nobody,' she lied, flattening out her legs so Otis could set the tray down on her lap, and picking up the spoon. He regarded her, his eyebrows knitting together a bit.

'If it's that moron Nate, I'm gonna box him upside—'

Nova held up a hand, shaking her head. 'Absolutely not. And no boxing upside anything, all right? That's done.'

'Yeah, OK,' Otis said warily, and she couldn't help thinking it was pretty sweet of her brother to care, let alone want to take up on her behalf with Nathan. *Ugh!* In the joy of hooking up with Sam, Nova had managed not to think about her ex for a good week or so. She was trying extra hard not to ruin the excitement of her summer with Sam by getting paranoid again.

Her phone began to ring, making her jump. She reached for it eagerly, and Otis pulled a *seriously?* face. But it was Gemma. Even though maybe she'd been secretly hoping for it to be Sam, Nova was equally excited to see her bestie's name flashing on the screen.

'Babe!'

'Babe!' Gemma replied, and they both laughed. 'I'm back, *chica*! Oh, and, uh, I'm downstairs!'

'Aw, amazing!' Nova said.

'Let me in, *por favor*!'

Nova coughed, and glanced up towards her brother, who was already heading out of the room. 'I'm bedridden, hon, I've got the flu, can you believe?' she said into her phone. 'I'm sending Ots down.' Nova opened her eyes wide and imploringly towards her brother. 'Can you let Gems in?' she said to him, and his expression went from annoyed to more amenable when he heard the specifics of the task. Without further argument, he headed downstairs, and Nova could have sworn she saw him check his appearance in the mirror next to her bedroom door before he jogged down.

She was beginning to get irritated at hearing Gemma and Otis chattering at one another, taking their sweet time, when her friend finally filled her doorframe.

'*¡Hola amiga!*' Gemma shouted, and launched herself on to Nova's bed, cuddling her while they both giggled. 'Oh, actually you know what, I'm not about catching your mucus right now,' she said, releasing Nova and retreating to the little chair in the corner.

'So you had an amazing time in Mexico, right?' Nova enquired, though she could already tell the answer was yes. They'd been in touch, but fairly intermittently, in the couple of weeks since Gemma had jetted off.

'Mate. It was ah-mazing. The weather, the culture . . . The boys,' she added with a grin. Nova rolled her eyes, though the mention of Spanish-speaking hotties did make her think of Sam again, and the little pepperings of the language that he used. It actually made Nova's insides flip.

How embarrassing!

She had only barely hinted at the turn of events with him to her best friend, but she knew they'd get to all that soon.

'So, pressies,' Gemma was saying, pulling her bag on to her lap and rummaging inside it determinedly.

'You didn't have to—' Nova began, but resistance was, of course, futile.

'I met this amazing woman who has an all-woman mariachi band. So, I got you one of their albums, coz I know you'll love it . . .' She frisbeed a CD on to the bed. 'Ooh, and I promise the last thing is no big deal, but I thought it was so cute.' She handed a little framed picture over – it was a reproduction of a painting that Nova knew was by Mexican artist Frida Khalo, one of her favourite artists. It showed the artist in a red shawl, holding hands with her husband, another famous Mexican artist, Diego Rivera. 'I took *copious* video for you to watch later of Casa Azul, and their studios and stuff, like I promised!' Casa Azul was Frida's little blue house, which had become a museum. Nova had introduced Gemma to Frida's work a while ago, and she loved her too. Nova had been *especially* jealous about this part of Gemma's trip! But it just showed how amazing a friend Gemma was that she had gone to all that trouble. 'I really thought that pic shows, like, the possibility of romance.' Gemma looked a bit wistful, and Nova set her tray of soup aside to shuffle to the edge of the bed, closer to her friend.

'All right, hon?'

Gemma nodded, and Nova reached over to squeeze her hand. 'Yeah. Yeah, actually! I mean, Wanda, my dad's new . . . whatever . . . did come for part of the trip, but it was OK. She's not entirely terrible, I suppose. I'm doing my best to keep the faith with this love stuff!' Nova thought Gemma glanced towards the door – and Otis – as she said that. Then her white teeth sparkled as she spread a smile Nova's way. 'Speaking of which. *How* are we not talking about that gorgeous American right now?'

Nova shuffled back to lean against her headboard again, and took a deep breath. She knew her expression was already giving away her happiness, but Gemma was emphatic about her not skipping a single detail. Nova filled her friend in on everything that happened at Summer Fields, and bashfully showed her the video of the performance with Sam. Even though Gem had already spotted it, she had held off on asking about the details until they could be face to face. Nova laughed (and coughed) as Gemma feigned a heat-induced faint, fanning herself dramatically.

'It's even spicier the second time. Babe, your laptop is going to melt from all that hot, hot chemistry!' she said, swiftly followed by, 'OK, I'm watching it again!' When the video finished the second time, Gemma's face was still awestruck. 'Nova, you are *unbelievably* good. Seriously. I'm not surprised he was completely overwhelmed! So when are you going to see him again?'

Nova closed her laptop, curving her lips dejectedly. 'Probably not 'til we go to WildArts –

he's in Madrid and then I think Barcelona, hanging out with his dad while he works over there.'

'Must be nice!' Gemma said.

'OK, Ms Just Got Back From Mexico!' Nova said with a chuckle, tossing a throw-pillow at her friend.

Gemma caught it. 'Point taken. But still, it's good in a way. Gives you time to get over this whole –' she gestured to Nova's coughing self, the strewn tissues and the soup bowl – 'situation,' she finished, scrunching her nose up in disgust, and then yelping as Nova decided on throwing a balled-up tissue this time. Only her phone beeping with a message saved Gem from further onslaught, as Nova saw Sam's name on the screen. But her excitedly lifted eyebrows fell as she opened up his message.

Selfie time, beautiful! I miss your face. I need to see it ASAP. Hit me back. ;)

He'd accompanied it with a devastatingly hot

picture of himself on a sun-soaked balcony in Madrid. Even though he was pulling a joking faux-model expression, he looked gorgeous – his skin a deep brown, his curly hair messy, his white T-shirt pristine.

'What?' Gemma asked, and Nova turned the screen towards her. Gemma rolled her eyes. '*Oh, my new boyfriend is soooo good-looking I'm upset,*' she mocked, laughing.

'Read the message, hon. How can I take a selfie looking this rough?'

Gemma shrugged. 'Send an old one!' she said.

'I don't take any!' Nova retorted, then blew her nose. Gemma swiped Nova's phone out of her hands and scrolled through her photos.

'Wow, yeah, you really don't,' she said, with an incredulous chuckle. 'OK, we can do this. Fake it 'til you . . . don't have the flu.'

Nova submitted to Gemma's art direction, expert filter-application and judicious camera angles, and several pictures later, she managed to send a picture back while they both giggled. Sam's response was almost embarrassingly enthusiastic, saying he'd been inspired to write another song about her on the basis of the selfie.

'Ugh, you've seriously secured a good one here, Nov,' Gemma said dreamily, but suddenly Nova began to worry. After all, Sam couldn't be for keeps, could he? He lived in America. If this was what it was like when he was in Spain for a week or so, what would happen when he had to go back to Miami?

CHAPTER 17

A couple of days and several bowls of boil soup and yucky paracetamol drinks later, Nova was almost back to fighting fitness. And not a moment too soon – she was concerned she'd have to referee the scene unfolding in front of her!

The sun was finally setting outside on the busy Brixton streets, but inside Eats & Beats everything, and everyone, was still – except Grandma Rosalind, who was chewing vigorously with her eyes closed, her face contemplative. Her dark skin shone with the radiance of having just returned from her summer trip back home to Sierra Leone, and she was sporting a new bright blue-and-pink patterned dress, one of several she'd had made while she was over there. Before her sat many different bowls of food: chicken, grilled fish, stews and side dishes. Nova knew her mum and dad had been working non-stop to refine their menu of planned submission dishes for the Street to Elite competition. The finals were only days away, taking place at WildArts. This one wasn't just a music festival; literature and culinary arts were also part of the entertainment. But no matter how certain the customers, and Nova and Otis, had been about the deliciousness of the food their parents been working on, everyone knew that it was Grandma Rosalind's opinion that would truly give the seal of approval.

She swallowed now, her brows knitting. She took a swig of homemade ginger beer, then drew a deep breath. Nova looked at her mum. Her mum looked at Nova's dad. Dad looked at Otis. Then they all returned their gaze to Grandma Rosalind. She looked back . . . and then broke out into peals of laughter.

'Deana, darling? Hector? It is . . . It's sweet, o! Seriously, seriously good. You will win, I tell you no lie!'

They all laughed too, breathing a collective sigh of relief as Grandma raised her ample figure from the table to give her daughter and son-in-law a hug. Nova was glad her grandma had reassured her parents that their hard work had paid off. She still had a slight concern bubbling away in the back of her mind about the restaurant, and what she'd heard her mum saying about the rates. Hopefully a win at the competition would make things more secure. The food really was delicious, but there would be some tough competition at the festival.

They all served up more food, and Nova was glad to have some chilled time to spend with her family before another hectic trip with the food truck. But at the same time, she was absolutely dying to get on the road the next day – because she was only a few hours away from seeing Sam again!

 228

The anticipation felt even more extreme than waiting for Grandma's thumbs-up!

Nova was awake before her alarm the next morning, scampering eagerly to the bathroom so that she could beat her brother to it. She wanted to make sure she was looking and feeling her best for her long-awaited reunion with Sam. But as she passed Otis' bedroom, she heard a phlegmy cough. She knocked cautiously on his door, and saw her brother squinting at the bright sunlight already filtering in through his thin curtains, shielding his eyes.

'You all right, Ots?' she enquired.

He struggled to sit up. 'Err, about that flu you had . . . Were you, like, feverish?'

She frowned. 'Yeah.'

'Shaky? Cough like Dad's old motor?'

Uh-oh. 'Yep.'

'Head pounding like someone's putting on a

rave in your skull?'

'Oh, Ots. Sorry, mate.'

But not as sorry as she would be! There was no way her family could skip the festival, obviously, but if Otis wasn't able to come, it would mean *double* the duty for Nova – and way less time with Sam. Still, she knew her brother felt bad, and not just because of the flu. He wasn't one to shirk his duties unless he really had to.

Her mum and dad were already packing the van downstairs when Nova told them about her brother. After sorting Otis out with some of her leftover medicine, TV series recommendations to stream, and giving Grandma a call to come and look after him while they were away, Nova and her parents set off for WildArts festival.

Even though she'd messaged Sam rather glumly explaining that her time would likely be once again monopolised by the food truck, he had come back straight away telling her that he was glad to spend whatever time he could with her. She smiled down at her phone, but was careful not to call too much attention to her 'mooning', as Otis had called it. She was definitely not interested in getting the third degree from her parents about Sam just yet!

Luckily her mum was concentrating on driving the van, while her dad cranked up his favourite reggae tunes on the stereo. The sun was radiant, but Nova had packed her wellies just in case – she wasn't taking any chances this time. The festival was only a couple of hours' drive from London, and smaller than the last two they'd been to. But the beautiful site felt like another world as they pulled in. It was filled with little grottos, a big, calm lake, and cute wooden bridges. WildArts felt like a fairy-tale world – well, one with banging music and really cool speakers giving talks!

Deana effortlessly navigated the big, colourful truck into its spot in the catering area, and Nova welcomed the chance to stretch her legs before helping to unload things. The campsite for the catering staff was next to the food area this time, and her dad even offered to set up the tents.

'Yeah, that's all well and good when there are only two to set up this time,' Nova told him with a laugh.

But soon enough they were settled in, and Nova was itching to call Sam and see if he had arrived on site yet. It seemed likely if his dad was working there. But when she finally got a chance to try him away from her parents' prying ears, his phone rang and rang to no answer. She typed a message to ask if he was there, but while she could see he'd read it, after several minutes there was still no reply.

'Is he seriously leaving me on *read*?' Nova said to herself, frowning. This was exactly the kind of needy feeling she didn't want, but she couldn't help tapping the icon for Instagram on her phone while she waited for Sam to respond. Maybe she'd see a pic of him at the festival already, like she had before . . . ? But there was nothing suggesting he was there. As she scrolled through the photos and videos on his feed, she noticed that one account had been through and commented some flirtatious remark on practically every single one.

MIAMI_Belinda: OMG thirst trap and I am PARCHED.

MIAMI_Belinda: Wow, sing me to sleep @SamRodriguezMusic

MIAMI_Belinda: Call me ♥

MIAMI_Belinda: Our song xx

Wow, and Nova had been worried *she* was a little too into Sam's page. This girl was way over the top. Nova clicked through to her feed and saw a barrage of pouting selfies from a Kardashian-a-like dark-haired girl who was clearly from Miami too.

'Probably just a classmate, or some random Insta-chick with way too much time on her hands trying to get likes,' Nova told herself quietly, even as alarm bells began to ring. She silenced them quickly – she wasn't interested in being paranoid about Sam. Besides, he was getting more followers by the hour. He was clearly becoming popular, and Nova was glad for him. His music was amazing, and frankly, he *was* incredibly hot. Who wouldn't be excited by his pics? Plus, she was the only one who knew that a couple of those songs he'd posted were all about her.

As if on cue, her phone finally began to ring, with Sam's name flashing on the screen. She tried to let it ring a few times before answering, so as not to seem *too* eager.

'Hi,' she said.

'Hey, beautiful,' he replied, and she blushed. 'Sorry, we were delayed coming back from Spain so I only just got back to London.' He sounded a bit tense.

'No worries. Everything OK?'

She heard Sam sigh on the other end of the phone, and really wished he were there so she could see his face, maybe help make him smile at least. 'Yeah, just . . . I kind of thought me and my pops were going to be out there just us, and in Madrid we were getting to a pretty good place. But then his girlfriend wound up "needing" to meet us in Barcelona. It never feels like she's genuinely interested in him, just whatever she can get out of him, you know? And honestly, sometimes I worry about his sobriety around her, Nov. I mean, what if things end up back like how they were before?'

Nova listened, her heart squeezing for him. 'I know it's tough. But at least your dad's made some effort to make amends, right? He'll be fine, I reckon.' She felt a bit ill-equipped to talk about it, but she wanted to try and help.

'I don't know,' Sam said, still sounding a bit dejected. 'I'm not totally sure I trust him not to disappoint me again. Us, our family . . .'

She wasn't sure how to respond. Could people really change? Her mind wandered to Nathan, and how hurt she had been with that whole situation. It was nowhere near the same thing, but it was hard to imagine someone capable of causing any kind of heartbreak would change their ways. Nova didn't want to sound too jaded though.

'I wish you were here already so we could talk about this more in person,' she said earnestly, and she could sense the smile from Sam now even through the phone.

'Me too, believe me. But I'll be there tomorrow, and I'm coming straight to you.'

'Can't wait,' she said softly.

CHAPTER 18

Nova felt a wave of smugness hit her along with the deliciously warm water from the *clean*, eco-filtered shower. She'd sweet-talked the lady who was running an area of specially sectioned-off bathroom facilities into letting her and her parents use them for the next couple of days in exchange for free food, and it was definitely worth it. After drying off and dressing in a Gemma-approved fringed tank top and black shorts, she felt ready to hit the food truck and wait for Sam to come and sweep her off her feet. But when she strolled over to Eats & Beats, she saw her parents glancing at one another nervously as they prepared their new breakfast roti wraps, ready for the eager queue of customers that was beginning to form.

'Sorry I'm late, guys. That shower was too good, innit?'

'Mmm hmm,' her dad replied, still seeming distracted. 'Err, yeah, thanks for sorting that, sweetheart.'

Nova raised an eyebrow at her parents as she tied on her apron and started cracking eggs into a bowl. 'OK, spill it,' she said, trying to sound light-hearted even though she worried this was finally going to be the rent-and-rates-problem talk. 'What's going on?'

Her mum finished handing over a wrap to a burly security guy, her customer-service smile fading as she turned to Nova. 'It's the preliminary round of Street to Elite at the culinary tent today. They changed the timings, so now it's at half twelve. Smack in the middle of lunch service!'

Hector nodded. 'I guess we'll have to shut

the truck down, but that means we miss a whole lot of takings . . .'

Nova knew they needed to make every day at the festival count, especially if there were financial challenges back at the restaurant. 'I can handle it,' she said confidently, even though she knew holding down the fort at the truck by herself on the busy first day of WildArts was going to be nigh-on impossible. Not to mention that it meant even *less* time to see Sam even if he did come and see her today.

'I don't think so, Nov,' her mum was saying, but Nova shook her head emphatically, pausing to tie up a stray loc. Then something occurred to her, and she grinned.

'No, trust me it will be fine,' she said. Well, she hoped so. 'One sec.'

She jogged down the back steps of the truck and pulled her phone out of her pocket. Quickly, she tapped out a message.

OK, so how are your culinary skills? Or at least

your maths/coin counting abilities? I'm looking for a hero . . .

She quickly followed up with a voice-note explaining the dilemma to Sam, who sent back a picture of himself with a sweatshirt tied around his neck like a cape, hands on his hips as he stared off into the distance like Superman.

A hero, you say? I'll be that for you x

She grinned goofily at his message, quickly popping her phone away when her mum stuck her head out of the back to see what she was up to. 'Phone can wait, Nov! We've got hungry punters here!'

'Sorry, Mum,' Nova said, heading back into the truck. 'Just securing our rescue!'

Deana pulled out more organic vegetables from the rack above their heads. 'Is that so?' she asked, beginning to chop more onions and peppers for the wraps. Nova concentrated on whipping the eggs she'd cracked, seasoning them with her other hand.

'Yeah,' she said, smiling as she beat the mixture. 'A friend of mine who I met a few weeks ago at Summer Fields. His name's Sam.' Her mum was silent until Nova looked up and saw Deana's appraising smile.

'Mmm *hmm*. A friend, eh?'

Nova flared her nostrils and ignored her. She was just excited about having figured out a way to spend time with Sam *and* help out her parents!

Nova had spent a good fifteen minutes reassuring her mum and dad that everything would be fine at the truck, and wishing them a ton of luck with the preliminary round of Street to Elite. She was kind of gutted she couldn't be there, but she had every faith in their success. They'd agreed to shut the truck for an hour between eleven and midday so that Nova wouldn't have to contend with late-riser festival-goers looking for some pre-lunchtime grub. But at five minutes to twelve, her parents had left to head to the competition, and Nova was nervously checking and re-checking the food prep, making sure the till had change over again – and glancing anxiously at her phone. Still no sign of Sam, no message, nothing. He said he'd be there at quarter to . . .

But as she was writing the specials on the chalkboard on the front of the truck, she felt a strong arm wrap around her waist, and a familiar, deep voice in her ear.

'Someone order a hero?'

Nova felt every cell of her body tingle, but tried to make her voice sound stern. Continuing to write on the board she said, 'Honestly, you can't get the staff these days, eh? Time do you call this?' She span around, and Sam held on to her waist as he gave her his most apologetic look, pouting and batting his long, dark lashes adorably. Her heart skipped a beat at finally seeing his gorgeous face again. He edged closer, closing his eyes and then eagerly pressing his lips against her mouth. Nova completely forgot she was even meant to be working as he continued the kiss . . .

They were interrupted by someone coughing.

'You lot open or what?' asked a slim boy dressed in muddy black boots and a unicorn onesie. Nova and Sam broke apart, laughing.

'Yep!' said Nova. 'Give me two minutes, yeah?'

She grabbed Sam's hand, pulling him around the back and into the truck. He tried to kiss her again, but much as it pained her, she pressed one hand to his strong chest to push him gently away. 'Uh uh uh,' she said teasingly. She grabbed an Eats & Beats apron off a hook and thrust it towards him. '*You* are about to get a crash course in fusion cuisine, young Samuel!'

Sam was actually a very quick learner, though Nova mainly kept him on the till and on microwave or chopping duty where needed. The unicorn boy had been quickly joined by a big group of his mates, and from there the line at Eats & Beats grew and grew. Sam kept up a lively patter with the crowd, drumming up even more business.

'Didn't I tell you this place can't be beat?' he said as a pair of blonde girls came back to buy some more ginger beer to wash down their jerk 'n' jollof bowls – and, Nova suspected, to flirt with Sam. She wasn't jealous, though. Every opportunity he'd got to brush against her hip, run a fingertip down her arm, or peck her cheek with a kiss, he had definitely taken. She was exhausted from the work, but with every passing minute she felt like she was falling for Sam Rodriguez more and more. It was hot in that truck, that was for sure – and not just from the heat of the cooking!

At last, it was heading for four o'clock, the time when her parents had agreed it might be worth Nova winding things up at the truck and closing up until six, when they would be back and dinner service would start. Nova had Sam sweeping up and cleaning surfaces while she wrapped up the last of the prepped food. Finally, she closed up the hatch at the front of the truck, and exhaled. She knew her parents were due back any minute, but she was powerless to resist when Sam cranked up the music and pulled her in close in the small space inside the truck, now that they were shielded from view. The song he played was one of her favourite Nina Simone tunes, 'Baltimore', with its lilting reggae-influenced beat, and she was doubly impressed when Sam started singing along in her ear as he swayed them from side to side. She felt like she was floating on a cloud . . .

But she came crashing down as she heard her parents' voices outside.

Quicker than lightning, she sped out the back of the truck. 'Hey! So . . . How did it go?' she asked, genuinely dying to know. She studied her parents' faces eagerly, but their expressions were giving nothing away – except perhaps curiosity as Sam emerged behind her, still wearing his apron.

'Mrs Clarke, Mr Clarke? I'm Sam Rodriguez. We've semi-met before, because I've already been here as a customer. I am a *huge* fan of your food. Like, it's embarrassing – she'll tell you,' he said, placing a hand on Nova's shoulder. Then he glanced at Nova's dad, and swiftly removed it again. Instead, he reached out and shook Hector and Deana's hands, giving them a charming smile that Nova could tell was already winning her parents over.

'Nice to meet you, Sam. And thank you so much for helping Nov out today, you have no idea how much of a life-saver that was. We'll give you a little something to say thank you,' her mum said, heading into the truck and towards the till.

'No, no, absolutely not,' Sam told her quickly, and Nova beamed at him. But she still hadn't had an answer from her parents.

'OK, the suspense is killing me. Tell me what happened with the competition!'

Nova's dad took a deep breath. 'Well . . . we made it! We're in the finals!'

She shrieked in excitement, then hugged her dad tightly, followed by her mum, who was emerging back out of the truck clutching a piece of cake. 'Easy, easy, we haven't won yet!' she said. 'Anyway, Sam, please at least take some of

Hector's famous rum cake, eh?'

Sam took the wrapped package gladly. 'Thank you so much, Mrs C,' he said, fixing her with his broadest, most mum-pleasing smile. 'Actually, I was wondering. Could I steal Nova away for a couple hours? I promise I'll have her back here for dinner service.'

'Of course! You two have been working really hard.' Nova didn't miss the pleased look her mum gave her, and prayed that she wouldn't do or say anything embarrassing. 'Thanks again. Have a good time!'

Nova and Sam said bye to her parents and walked away, shoulder to shoulder. When they were comfortably out of view, she took Sam's hand. 'Extremely good parent-wrangling, Rodriguez!' she said, grinning up at him.

Sam held up his free palm in protest. 'Hey, that was all genuine. I had a ton of fun today, and your parents are really cool.' His expression turned sly. 'But now that I have you to myself for a couple hours, I don't know about you but I could do with

cooling down after all that heat in the truck . . .'
His eyes seared into hers, and Nova wasn't sure
that it would ever be possible to cool down around
him! 'How 'bout a dip in the lake?' he finished.

'Err . . . Not sure about that. I don't have a
costume with me, and I'm pretty sure skinny
dipping isn't the done thing, especially not at a
crowded festival in the middle of the afternoon.'

Sam pulled her closer to him as they walked.
'OK, I'm going to need a second to get over that
imagery,' he said, smiling down at her, but then
guided her towards the lake anyway. 'I've already
scoped out someplace that could help us out.' He
pointed towards a cute little hut next to the lake
that was selling swimming costumes, inflatables
and other bits and bobs. 'My treat!'

Nova let go of his hand to head towards the
shop, but then spun back to face Sam. 'OK,' she
said, 'but I'm not letting you pick the swimsuit.
Skimpy bikini is a no-go.'

'What if I wore one, too?' he asked with a grin.

Nova pretended to consider it, though it did

suddenly occur to her that she would soon be seeing that perfect body of Sam's up close and in swimming shorts.

After a few minutes of browsing, both of them had picked out costumes. Sam paid for them, along with two big bright towels with the WildArts logo emblazoned on them. Nova watched as he produced a credit card to pay for their goods, curious about how he was able to treat her to over-priced swimming gear. It was none of her business, but she just hoped Sam wasn't overstretching himself to impress her.

She quickly let it go as they made their way back out into the warm sunshine and put their stuff into one of the lockers in the lakeside swimming huts. Nova ducked into a changing cubicle and put on her new swimming costume, then stepped outside. There was a wooden promenade jutting out into the lake, which sparkled in the warm afternoon sunshine. People everywhere were splashing and laughing, and music was being pumped loudly across the water.

Nova could feel Sam's eyes on her as he emerged from the men's changing room. She hung her towel on a nearby tree, revealing the neat orange one-piece swimsuit she'd picked out. It was all she could do not to ogle him, too. His broad brown chest had a light dusting of hair, and he looked athletic in his blue board shorts.

'I bet it's cold in there,' Nova said, trying to break the tension. Sam took her hand in his and wove his fingers in between hers.

'So I say we just leap and hope,' he said, looking at her closely.

'You and your inspirational messages,' she replied, hoping to lighten the tone. But she really did want to take a leap of faith with Sam. Before she knew it, he was pulling her into a run, their hands still interlinked, and they raced down the promenade laughing. Then they sailed into the air, hung there for what felt like for ever . . . and landed in the lake with a huge splash, to a few cheers from those nearby.

Nova burst back up to the surface, still

chuckling giddily as she shook out her locs. Sam swam over to her, his handsome face accentuated as his hair was slicked back with the water. He pulled her into an embrace, and she kicked to stay afloat, though again it felt like hardly any effort. Because before she knew it, Sam was kissing her again . . .

Nova knew she was going to find saying goodbye to Sam more and more difficult with every passing day. But for now, in that moment, everything was perfect.

CHAPTER 19

Nova exhaled hard as she sat down on the little metal steps that led out of the food truck, wiping her hands on her apron. She glanced at her phone, hardly believing that it was already three o'clock in the afternoon. She saw a couple of messages from Gemma, and another from Sam. He'd tried to come by and say hello, but Nova had been flat-out serving people in the truck, so it was hard for her to find a moment to talk to him. Now she was finally able to grab a couple of hours before they got into dinner. She felt almost giddy as she hit dial on his number, but when he answered, he sounded distracted.

'Hey . . .'

'Hi,' Nova said. 'So guess what? I have approximately one hour and fifty minutes free before I have to get back behind the grill. What are you up to?' She heard voices in the background, and Sam pulled away from the phone to say he'd be there in a minute.

'Uh, I actually kind of said I'd head to this thing with my dad . . .' Sam said, sounding reluctant.

Nova didn't want to get in the way of Sam spending some time with his father, especially after what he had told her before. 'Oh. OK, no, you should definitely do that. There's loads I can go and check out. Hopefully we can meet up later this evening?'

'For sure,' Sam replied. 'I'll hit you up later. Bye, beautiful.'

He'd hung up before she could even say goodbye properly herself. She tried not to sigh too hard as she looked at her phone screen fading to black. She didn't need to be joined at the hip with Sam, and it wasn't a lie – there was lots of cool stuff to check out at the festival.

'Comin' through,' her dad said behind her, making her jump. Nova stood up from the steps and undid her apron.

'What you up to, girl?' he said. 'Fancy coming to check out a talk in the Lecture tent with me? Norman Jay is giving a chat about sound systems, so you know I have to go check that out, and your mother's off to some chair massage thing.'

Nova smiled – she knew the famous DJ was one of her dad's heroes. If Sam was hanging out with his dad, why shouldn't she spend a bit of time with hers? 'Yeah, sounds good!' she said.

A few minutes later they set off, following the map towards the small tent where the talks were taking place. On the way, Nova even persuaded her dad to pose for a selfie, grinning as they put their faces together in the warm sunshine. Nova chuckled at how similar they looked with their locs piled on their heads and their deep brown skin. She popped on to Instagram quickly to post the picture, but again she couldn't help noticing that MIAMI_Belinda girl lurking in the mentions under Sam's latest post, too – a quick video of him in front of the lake. She felt a weird mixture of relieved and a bit put out that he'd posted it with no mention of her having been there, too.

Nova tried to put it out of her mind as they arrived at the tent. It seemed buzzy and surprisingly full, and she didn't want to judge, but the people inside didn't necessarily seem like big fans of sound system culture. A lot of them seemed more likely to be into middle-of-the-road rock, like . . .

'Flightpath fans!' A lady wearing a flowing floral dress was at the microphone, reading something from a piece of paper. 'We've got a treat in store for you! I know a lot of you have already heard about this on the grapevine, but we're rejigging the running order here today. We've been lucky enough to persuade the fabulous Clay Cooper to come and talk to us a bit about his new memoir, *Path to Peace*, before he heads to the main stage for an exclusive acoustic solo set. He'll be here in just a few minutes,' she said, glancing off to the side of the stage to nod at someone. The woman sounded fit to burst with excitement, but Nova glanced at her dad, pressing her lips into a flat line.

'Really?' she enquired, hoping Hector might decide they should go and check out something else, but he shrugged.

'Couple of their songs aren't too bad, you know,' he told her, and she rolled her eyes. 'I think he could be interesting!' her dad protested. 'With any luck we catch a bit of Norman Jay, too, before we have to head back?'

Grudgingly, Nova edged her way through the crowded tent with her dad, and they managed to find two empty seats. Clearly word about Clay Cooper was spreading fast, because soon it was standing room only. A moment later, the woman bustled back towards the microphone, beaming.

'Ladies and gents, it's the moment we've all been waiting for – we're so pleased to welcome to the stage . . . the fantastic Mr Clay Cooper!'

The audience went wild as a tall, bronzed man with longish, light-brown hair that had a typically 'rock star' greasy-but-expensive look to it, strode across the stage to where two armchairs had been set up on a worn rug. The lady took the other seat, and a stage hand dressed all in black rushed on, crouching down as if nobody would notice him, to hand Clay Cooper a microphone.

'Awright?' he said as he gripped it, and the crowd cheered again. 'Pleasure to be here, thanks a lot for having me.' His voice was gravelly and deep, his accent a mixture of cockney and transatlantic. His eyes crinkled handsomely at the corners, and sort of did make Nova warm to him a bit as he smiled. As the host began her interview, Nova had to admit that Clay was coming across well – funny, self-deprecating. His humour actually kind of had a charm to it. When he was invited to read an extract from his memoir, Nova felt a bit of a weird lump form in her throat. He read a section about the birth of his first child.

'. . . I named him Yosemite, and I pushed hard

for that name,' he said towards the end of the passage, looking up from the book with a smile. 'His mother took some convincing, and I know he hates it. But like that incredible national park in the US, with its mountains and trees, holding Yo in my arms for the first time, he felt like the most beautiful thing I'd ever seen.' Clay finished the reading and was quiet for a moment, and the host let him absorb his thoughts again while the audience clapped.

'That was really lovely,' she said. 'And how do you feel about family now?'

Clay closed the hardback book with his black and white photograph on the cover, and looked down at his lap for a while longer before he answered. 'I love my kids, but as you'll see in the book, I wasn't the best dad or husband for a long time. You know, I'm working on it. For a long time there, it was pretty dark. Addiction is something that I'm in recovery from, so it was tough. Hard as it was, I think the divorce really was the best thing for everyone . . .'

He tailed off, and the hostess nodded empathetically. Nova did admire his honesty, and she could tell it must be a hard thing to talk about. Again she felt the gratitude for her own family and how close they were, especially when she considered the complexities Gemma and Sam had faced with their parents splitting up.

Thinking about Sam, Nova's heart flipped and slightly sank, remembering how she hadn't been able to hang out with him that afternoon, and her worries about that stupid girl on his Instagram. She wanted to try and find a chance to talk to him about what he thought might happen come the end of the summer. After all, there were only one or two festivals left in the calendar, so it was likely she'd be running out of time with him soon. At least CityFest was taking place in London, and with any luck between now and then Sam would be around in town more for them to hang out. But what would happen when he went back to Miami?

Nova returned her attention to the stage, and saw that Clay was smiling off to the wings, seeming lighter-hearted. 'But now, of course, I have my beautiful girlfriend Sadie, and I reckon a bloke only gets that lucky a couple of times in his life, so I'm keeping myself on the straight and narrow!'

The hostess seemed to light up at the mention of Sadie Varma, and Nova remembered Gemma talking about her and Clay being together. 'Ah, the gorgeous Sadie,' the lady said. 'There have been engagement rumours swirling—'

'Swirling, indeed!' Clay deflected good-naturedly, though Nova could tell he was not interested in going there. The interviewer looked down to the front of the audience, to where Nova spotted a woman with a short, black bob – probably from a PR company – shaking her head.

'Err . . .' the host bumbled, but Clay swooped in to rescue her.

'One thing that I *have* been focussing on lately is taking care to give back. Especially in terms of the planet, you know, the environment. It's tough – we take a lot of flights, and touring has a big impact, but I've been working with a great new start-up company, developing ways to off-set what we do in that regard . . .' He began to talk about some of the initiatives, and actually sounded quite knowledgeable. Nova had to admit to herself that she might have judged him a bit too harshly. She may not be a fan of Flightpath's music, but there was something about Clay Cooper that she couldn't help but like.

Eventually the interview wrapped up, and Nova applauded along with the whoops and whistles from the rest of the audience. Clay waved and bowed jokingly, then jogged away off the stage.

'Seems like a good man,' her dad said.

'Yeah,' Nova agreed. Something occurred to her, and she turned in her seat to face Hector more. 'Dad . . . Do you ever wish you'd had more success with your music?' She watched as he scratched the bristles on his face a little bit, slightly worried she'd offended him.

Her dad drew in a breath. 'Of course. But that industry . . . Nova, it's rare that you can get any kind of success with it.' He looked regretful, but continued. 'It's full of snakes, too. I don't know how much I'd encourage anybody to get into it. I'm happy with just doing my little music on the side, and focussing on the restaurant. And that's why we want you and Otis to have your studies, to get you to where you need to be, too.'

Nova nodded, feeling resigned. He was right, it was so hard to get anywhere with music. That was a big part of why she felt like there wasn't much point in getting over her fears to share her own. Maybe it should just be something she did for herself.

She was jolted out of her thoughts as her dad glanced at his watch and said, 'Ah, I'd better be heading back to the truck.' The disappointment on her dad's face about missing his talk made Nova feel a bit glum, too. Her parents worked so hard to keep the business going strong. Hearing Clay talk about his darker times made Nova feel extra grateful towards her father and his stable, sensible ways.

'Nah, why don't you stay for a bit, Dad?'

she said. 'I can help Mum with the dinner prep. You deserve to catch a bit of the talk you actually came for!'

The lady running the stage was already announcing that the DJ would be with them in five minutes. 'Treat after treat!' she was saying excitedly to the crowd. 'Trust me, you don't want to miss this, another legendary music icon will be right here very soon, Mr Norman Jay, MBE . . . !'

It didn't take too much persuading for her dad to agree to Nova's offer.

But as she was trying to navigate her way out, she thought she spotted Sam in amongst the crowd outside the tent. Nova was about to open her mouth to call out to him, but then she noticed that he had been stopped to pose for a picture with someone. A girl. His arm slipped around the girl's waist in a way that, rationally, Nova knew was perfectly normal, but irrationally made her hot with a mixture of anger and jealousy. She cursed Nathan for making her feel so paranoid, but she couldn't help it – especially as she got closer and saw the girl peck Sam's cheek for the final picture her friend was excitedly taking.

'We saw you play at the Lumina tent at Summer Fields. You are, like, seriously talented,' Nova heard the photo girl saying as Sam pulled away from her. 'I reckon you'll be massive soon!'

'Massive, huh?' He patted his stomach jokingly. 'Appreciate that, thanks a lot,' he added, smiling his charming smile at the girls. Then his eye caught on Nova. He seemed to be a bit thrown at seeing her, but the smile remained on his face as the girls walked off, giggling and looking at the pictures on the phone.

'Nova?' Sam said, as she came to a stop in front of him. 'What are you doing here?'

'Could ask you the same thing,' Nova said, pushing her hands into the pockets of her cut-off denim shorts. Her sleeveless shirt left her arms exposed, which she silently cursed as Sam brushed a hand down one. Goosebumps spread where he touched her, but she looked up at him, awaiting an explanation. His hand dropped to his side at her expression. When he didn't say anything, she added, 'I thought you were busy doing something with your dad?'

'I was, but we finished up, so I was actually just headed to come find you at the truck . . .'

'You had to stop for your adoring fans, though,' Nova said. Even as she said it, she cringed at the accusatory tone of her voice. Sam looked at her, and for the first time since they'd met, he seemed irritated.

'Fans? They were just a couple of girls who'd seen me play. I appreciate anyone who's into what I'm trying to put out there,' he said. 'And I wasn't lying, Nova. I was with my dad. We just kind of had a fight, so I wanted to come see if we could hang out instead, which is what I had wanted to do anyway.' He exhaled. 'But if you're accusing me of lying, I mean, apparently *you* were hanging out here,' he glanced towards the tent from which she'd emerged, 'checking out a guy you claimed was a fraud.'

'That wasn't planned, and you could have done

with hearing Clay Cooper's talk, actually. It might've helped with all these arguments you're having with your dad. He's sorted out his relationship with his kids, whereas it sounds to me like *you're* almost going out of your way to not give your dad a chance to—'

'No offence, Nova, but you don't know anything about it,' Sam interjected, a frown between his brows. Then he sighed, the muscles in his jaw clenching as he looked down at her. Nova hated that they were arguing. But she remembered that she was meant to be on her way to help her mum out.

'Look, I've got to go, anyway. You can spend more time, here or online, with your fans or whatever they are.' *Why am I being so petty?* Nova berated herself even as the words left her lips.

She tried to move past him, but Sam stepped to the side, bending down to look into her face. 'What is that supposed to mean?'

'Nothing,' Nova muttered, then looked up at him, her voice still low. 'But I feel like you're not being straight with me, Sam. You say you're hanging out with your dad, fine, but then you're all weird and vague about it. And . . . you don't tell me where you're staying at the sites, like you don't want me around there. You don't even really say much about your life back home, apart from mentioning your mum and brother. For all I know, you've got a girlfriend back in Miami, and I'm just a summer fling while you *supposedly* patch things up with your dad.'

Sam looked like he'd been punched in the gut, and let out an incredulous 'huh'. 'You're accusing me of *cheating*? You're saying I'm being unfaithful to some totally fictional girl back home with you?'

Nova felt heat creep up her cheeks, and tears prickling in her eyes. She took a deep breath and blinked to get rid of them. 'I don't know. No,' she mumbled. 'Apparently I don't know anything, right? Look, I have to go.' She moved past him, wishing she could explain why she felt so insecure, wishing she could have time to patch things up with Sam, or for him to explain more about his fight with his dad. She *hated* that he felt like she wasn't able to understand him. That was probably why she'd picked this stupid fight in the first place.

Instead, Nova just hurried away with a sinking feeling like a ball of lead in the pit of her stomach.

CHAPTER 20

'Are you absolutely sure you have everything?' Nova's mum asked her dad nervously. It was the day of the Street to Elite final, and they had to cook like their lives depended on it. Maybe their business did, anyway, if Nova's suspicions about the rates-and-rent hike were true.

'Guys, I checked over your list again this morning, and went through everything in the cooler boxes. I promise you, it's all there,' Nova reassured them both, trying for a smile even though she'd been in a serious slump since her argument with Sam the previous afternoon. 'We should get over there, right? They said two o'clock.'

They had agreed to close the food truck for lunchtime today so that they had time to prep, and so that Nova was able to come and watch them participate in the final round of the competition. It was just as well, seeing as she definitely had a feeling Sam wouldn't be up for helping out this time.

Nova was feeling jittery herself as they made their way to the big white tent where Street to Elite was taking place. It was still being set up inside, but it was a lot fancier in there than most of the other tents, and Nova could see a few TV cameras dotted here and there. A blonde woman with a head-microphone bustled over to Nova and her parents as they arrived, carrying a tablet computer.

'Ah, Deana, Hector, fabulous. Shall we get you set up?' she said efficiently, turning even as she spoke and gesturing for them all to follow.

'How come there are cameras and stuff?' Nova

asked the lady, who looked over her shoulder with a smile.

'We're filming a segment for *Sunday Breakfast*, and we have a special surprise guest judge for this last round, so it's a bit of a bigger deal. We have waivers for you to sign . . .' She came to a halt at the shiny chrome kitchen area set up on a slightly raised stage at the front of the tent. There were two other sets of people from the other restaurants in the finals. Nova glanced at her mum, who widened her eyes with a mixture of what Nova could tell was both excitement and more nerves, and her dad grinned – he clearly liked the sound of being on TV!

'Who's the guest judge?' Hector asked eagerly.

The lady leaned in conspiratorially. 'It's Clay Cooper, from Flightpath!' she said.

Wow, he's everywhere! Nova thought.

With a slight roll to her eyes, the woman added, 'And he's insisted his girlfriend, Sadie something, helps with the judging, too. I think she's interested in starting a lifestyle company or something.

Anyway, I'll let you get set up and we'll be by with some paperwork in a minute. Good luck, guys!'

Nova started helping with unpacking the ingredients, while her parents went to say hello and wish the other finalists good luck. They'd all been working hard to get to this point. Nova already liked the sound of one of the other restaurant's food, run by an Indonesian mother–daughter team. Nova's own mum had raved about their light, fluffy bao buns. The other finalist restaurant was serving a vegan take on modern British fare, but regardless of their skills, she was convinced that Eats & Beats would be better by a mile. Nova just hoped that the judges would agree . . .

'OK, judges, we're now into the final round – dessert!' the host, a man who Nova had seen on weekend TV, announced eagerly. 'From Salt of the Earth we have a vegan chocolate torte with peanut butter and coconut milk sauce. Bali Bao are gracing us with an Indonesian spiced cake, and Eats & Beats have banana fritters with ginger ice cream. Tuck in!'

Nova's stomach rumbled from the delicious smells filling the tent. The judges were sitting off to one side of the stage, while the three competing groups each had their own cooking station on the other side of it. Big screens above the stage showed the audience what the cooks were doing in mouth-watering high definition. Nova had her brother on video call so that he and their grandma could watch the competition, and she held up her phone as the judges tasted the food. A restaurant critic from a national newspaper smiled as she tried each dish. Clay Cooper tucked in heartily, while Sadie Varma barely seemed to get anything on her spoon as she delicately nibbled the desserts. Nova held her breath as they each gave their judgements on the final rounds, to smatterings of applause from the audience. She listened in closely to the judges' thoughts on her parents' dessert.

'Mmm, really great mixture of flavours,' the food critic said, her spoon seeming to almost automatically dive back for one last taste of the ginger ice cream. Nova knew it was really delicious.

Clay was nodding enthusiastically. 'Totally agree. And I'm no expert but those fritters were *really* light. Tasty business!'

'And Ms Varma, your thoughts?' the host asked, holding a microphone over to Sadie.

'Yeah. Really nice,' she said in her light, breathy voice, smiling carefully as she seemed to notice the camera focus in on her. Nova sighed, worried her less emphatic judgment could impact on the final scores for Eats & Beats. The host announced that they should have the results shortly, and Nova felt her belly flip in anticipation. She turned her phone around and said she'd call Otis back when the judges had their verdict ready. Then, to distract herself, she messaged some updates to Gemma about the competition. She ignored her friend's enquiries about whether things had been a blissed-up love-fest with Sam. Nova also did her very best to resist the urge to look at Sam's social media feeds, or message him herself. She could apologise for her part in their argument, she knew that, but she also didn't want to fall back on her old ways and get drawn into a relationship that was destined not to work out. Maybe this was just a sign that they should leave well enough alone . . .

Still, after five minutes of being strong, Nova clicked on to Sam's Instagram, and felt oddly pleased that there were no new posts on there. At least that meant there were no more pics or vids for these other girls to be ogling.

Wow, jealousy is unattractive, Nova, she told herself.

Just then, the host returned to the stage to a round of applause, and her jealousy was replaced with a sharp thrill of adrenaline and fear.

'OK, ladies and gents, thank you so much for your patience. I'm very pleased to say, the judges have made their decision!'

He consulted with one of the production staff, and they set up to record the big announcement

 275

for the TV cameras. Nova got Otis back on the video call, and after a bit more of an introduction to camera, the host went over to the judges. Nova could hear her heart beating in her chest, and tried not to let her phone shake as she filmed.

'Now, it's the big moment – Clay Cooper, I believe you have the judges' decision?' the host said.

'I do, mate. So, here we go . . . In third place, we have . . . Salt of the Earth!'

The audience applauded, and Nova crossed her fingers in her lap.

'In second place . . .' Clay continued, looking out to the audience then over to the contestants. Nova held up her crossed fingers to her parents as she saw them seek her out in the crowd. '. . . It's Bali Bao!' he announced.

Nova let out a shriek of excitement and sprang to her feet as the audience applauded. In her joy, she could barely hear Clay as he announced, 'That means in first place, we have the excellent . . . Eats & Beats!' He had to raise his voice to continue.

'Not only was their food unbelievable, but the sustainable credentials of the restaurant were bang up to date. Well done, guys!'

The crowd cheered and clapped, nobody louder than Nova. She knew she was drawing attention to herself – and that video she was recording would be all over the place! – but her mum and dad were clinging on to each other and jumping up and down excitedly, and she was, too! The host beckoned Hector and Deana over to the centre of the stage, grinning.

'Congratulations, you two!' he said as eventually the crowd quietened for a moment. 'Now, this means that not only have you won a full kitchen refit with brand new equipment from our fantastic sponsors, Elite Kitchens UK . . .'

'*And* a promotional mention on my brand-new lifestyle website, *Sadie Varma Sparkle*,' Sadie interjected, pulling over the microphone Clay had been using to announce the win.

'Err, yes,' the host said. 'But most of all, you've won yourselves our grand prize of fifty . . .

thousand . . . pounds!' The crowd applauded again as he handed them a massive cheque.

'Ots, Grandma! We won! Isn't this amazing!' Nova shouted down the phone, giggling at their giddy faces on her screen as they shouted their excitement, too. 'We'll call you back in a bit, OK?'

As the host finally wrapped things up, Nova ran up to the front of the stage, where her mum and dad leaned down to give her a hug.

'You *so* deserve this!' she told them, wiping away a tear of pride and happiness. 'Ots and Grandma are thrilled, too! Also . . . like, how are you meant to pay that massive-sized cheque into the bank?' They all laughed, and Nova made sure to take a few pictures. She posted one to her Instagram, and grinned as her friends back home began to hit the like button on it, as well as a practical *essay* of excitement from Gemma under the post!

Her mum and dad agreed that there was no need to re-open the food truck before heading back to London the next day. They hung out at the competition tent for a while, popping a bottle of champagne, commiserating with the runners-up, and all sharing their food. Before they knew it, it was getting late. Nova wished so badly that she could let Sam know everything that had happened and patch things up, but she wasn't sure where she stood. She knew it was cowardly, but she didn't want to be the first one to reach out. She dodged her mum's questions about 'where that nice young Sam from the other day' had got to, mumbling something about him being busy.

Instead, she and her parents went to watch one of the headline acts, Seun Kuti – son of the legendary Afrobeat pioneer Fela Kuti – play with his band. Nova almost forgot her worries about Sam as they all danced and celebrated Eats & Beats' triumph. It really did feel like a dream come true that the concerns about the business were solved, and all through the incredible talent of her parents!

'We are absolutely knackered!' her mum said as they all made their way back to their campsite after the performance. 'I've never been so ready to hit that inflatable mattress!'

Nova laughed. She wasn't really tired, and it was only just getting to ten o'clock as her parents turned in for the night. Nova promised not to stray too far, but went to sit in a quiet spot nearby, where a clearing in the trees had been decorated with magical fairy lights. She'd brought a folding chair, her little mini keyboard, and the Dictaphone that Sam had got her, too. Pulling on her favourite hoodie, and making sure there wasn't anybody around, she switched on the keyboard in her lap and began to play some chords, experimenting with a few lyrics she'd been working on in her head. Inevitably, they were about Sam, and her worries about if there was a future with him. As she worked on it, she almost forgot where she was, singing a jazzy, Amy Winehouse-esque riff with more emphasis and heart as the song formed. She stopped to work out a new section, and suddenly heard the strumming of a guitar behind her, echoing what she had been playing.

Whipping around in surprise, she saw Sam standing nearby in the faint light from the string of little bulbs in the trees. 'Oh!' she exclaimed, her heart racing, and not only from the shock of him appearing behind her.

'*Lo siento*, I didn't mean to scare you,' he said, and then nodded to her little set-up with her keyboard. 'Nova, that was . . . unbelievably beautiful,' he added softly.

Nova turned back around, embarrassment mixing with pride at his assessment. 'I was just messing about,' she told him, hearing his footsteps as he came round to sit on a nearby tree stump, facing her. In the low light, Sam's cheekbones stood out even more, and the little yellow bulbs were picked out in his eyes, which settled on her. He was dressed in his dark zip-up hoodie. He looked, in short, delicious.

Sam stood his guitar up between his knees and shoved his hands into the pockets of his hoodie.

'I heard that your folks won the competition,' he said, smiling.

Heard? Oh, so he's been checking my Insta, too, Nova thought.

'Yeah, it's pretty amazing,' she volunteered, still eyeing him warily.

'I'm so happy it worked out,' he said, then drew a long breath. 'Nova . . . about yesterday. I was acting like a moron. I was just bummed out about the fight with my pops, and I shouldn't have said—'

'No, neither should I,' Nova interrupted quickly. 'I shouldn't have said any of that stuff . . . I had a bad break-up before. I got cheated on and I suppose I'm just still getting over all of that.'

Sam got up, leaning his guitar against the stump, and moved to sit on the ground right in front of Nova. He put his hands up on her knees, his palms warm on her bare skin as he looked up at her. His eyes were swimming with emotion.

'Nova, I'm really sorry we fought.'

Instinctively, she reached out and took his

face in her hands. 'I'm sorry too,' she said, with a slow smile. She leant forwards and her lips found his, her hands circling around his head to play in his hair.

'OK, fine. Forgiven,' Sam whispered as they finally broke apart. He chuckled softly, then leaned back, reaching for his guitar. 'Hey, play that thing you were working on again? I think I have an idea for the next verse . . .'

Nova picked up the Dictaphone, waving it at him with a smile, and played back what she'd been doing, glad that the lyrics were abstract enough that just maybe he wouldn't figure out the song was about him. Sam nodded, picking out more chords, and somehow they began to play the song together, with Sam melding his percussive style with Nova's jazzier feel, harmonising and beginning to improvise new lines when they got to where Nova had run out of ideas. It was . . . magical. Before she knew it, Nova realised they'd finished the whole song, and were playing it over again.

'Nova, I know I've said it before,' Sam said eventually, 'but you were made for this.'

She thought again about what her dad had said earlier at the talk. But she didn't want to get into her reservations about it all tonight. Not when she'd just worked things out with Sam, not when there was so much magic in the air. She ignored what Sam had said, though, and instead gently placed her keyboard on the chair as she stood up and moved next to him on the ground. Putting the hood of her sweatshirt up to cushion her head, she lay back wordlessly and looked over at Sam, then glanced up through the illuminated trees to the dark sky. She could just about make out the stars above them. She turned back to him.

'That's enough of that,' she said quietly, and he nodded. He put his guitar aside, and lay down beside Nova, lifting one arm so that she could rest her head on his chest. They both stared up at the sky, Nova loving the feel of Sam breathing next to her.

After maybe an hour but what felt like an eternity, Sam gently shook her – she had fallen asleep. 'Hey, beautiful,' he said softly. 'I should probably head before your mom and dad come looking for you.' Nova could hear the regret in his voice, and she felt it too. 'You leaving tomorrow?' he asked.

'Yeah,' she said, clearing her throat of sleep. 'My brother's not feeling well, so Mum and Dad are keen to set off early in the morning to get back.'

Sam smiled at her. 'Well, I'm going to let you to show me around your city when we're both back in London,' he said. 'So I'm going to see you real soon.'

'You're going to *let* me? How generous,' she joked, but she was basking in Sam's radiant grin.

Gradually they stood up, and Sam pulled her into a kiss, until she felt like she'd drift up out of her Doc Martens. Then, squeezing her into a tight hug, he whispered, 'I don't know how I'm going to leave you, Nova Clarke.'

She knew he wasn't just talking about the festival.

'Me neither,' she whispered back.

PART IV
CityFest

CHAPTER 21

Nova grabbed a dilapidated basket from just outside the entrance to the West African grocer's in Brixton market, and set about filling it with all her mum's requests – extra scotch bonnets, egusi, more okra, tins of calalloo, plantains. Her left bicep was aching by the time she got to the till.

'Eh, keeping well, Nova?'

'Yes, Aunty,' Nova said respectfully, smiling at Kadie, the lady who was quickly and expertly weighing the goods Nova had handed over.

'Take these, too,' Kadie said, winking as she added a small bag of chin-chin, delicious little

West African biscuits, to the eco-bag Nova had given her to pack the goods into. 'Just for you.'

'Mmm, thanks Aunty!' Nova said with a grin, as she paid. She rummaged in the bag as she walked away so that she could start snacking on the chin-chin on her way back to the restaurant. The sun was fiercely hot, and her parents had just got the permission they'd applied for from the council to put a couple of tables and chairs outside on the pavement. These, as well as every other table in the place, were full. Nova made her way through the busy restaurant to the kitchen, and began unpacking the food she'd bought.

'Ah, thanks sweetheart,' her mum said, stirring a giant pot of stew. They both turned around as they heard someone else come into the kitchen.

'Eh-eh, you see the restaurant?' Grandma Rosalind exclaimed, bustling her large frame over to kiss Nova, and then Deana. 'No get room to move!'

Nova grinned. 'It's great, isn't it, Grandma? Ever since Mum and Dad won Street to Elite it's been mad. Otis is upstairs looking into sorting out an online booking system!'

Grandma gripped Nova's mum's shoulders and squeezed them, even as she peered over one to inspect the pot she was working on. 'Smells good . . . Maybe more palm oil?'

Despite her turned back, Nova could imagine her mum's expression at that, and chuckled as she finished unpacking. She pulled her phone out of the pocket of her shorts as a message came through. It was Gemma, forwarding a tweet from none other than Sadie Varma. It mentioned the 'incredible winners' of the prize she judged, and of course then segued into another mention of her lifestyle website. Clay Cooper (or his social media team) had been posting about Eat & Beats' delicious food and green credentials, too. Nova had no doubt that was why their usual demographic of locals had branched out to foodie types who photographed every dish before they ate it.

Her dad had also had an email yesterday from

a newspaper that had posted a rave review of the restaurant a couple of weekends ago. The journalist who'd done the review had spoken to the newspaper's food supplement editor. He'd enjoyed the way Eats & Beats' menu had useful food and eco ideas on it, as well as a recipe to take away. The paper wondered if Nova's parents would be up for trying a monthly column in the Sunday food magazine supplement. It was all almost too much to take in, and while Nova did worry a bit that her parents were now working their fingers to the bone to keep up, the cash was rolling in and the business was definitely not in any danger of being unable to afford the rent any more. Her parents had even suggested they might be able to hire more staff, so that Nova and Otis could concentrate fully on their studies after the summer break ended. Though thinking of the summer ending again made Nova blue, imagining the start of her A levels with no Sam in sight . . .

'My grandchild! Come talk to your grandmother,' Rosalind said, pulling Nova by the hand out the back door of the kitchen, despite her protestations that she should probably help her mum. 'Your father will be back in a minute, not a problem,' her grandma insisted with a smile. She settled heavily down on the old dining chair she always positioned just outside the door to soak up the sun in the summer months, and Nova sat on the little wall off to the side of it. 'So, your mum told me you saw the great Fela's son at this little festival? Aahh, the way we used to dance to his father!' She stood up a little and shook her amble waist from side to side to demonstrate, grinning.

Nova laughed. 'Yes, Grandma!' she said approvingly. 'Yeah, Seun Kuti was amazing.' Her grandmother had sat back down, and was looking over at her slyly.

'And she mentioned a young man was sniffing around you, too . . . ?'

Nova flushed, pulling a face. 'I'm not sure I'd call it "sniffing around". Sam was just helping out!'

'Sam, eh? Sam . . .'

'Rodriguez,' Nova finished, and Grandma

Rosalind raised an eyebrow.

'He's Spanish?' she asked.

'Well, his mum's Cuban, his dad's English. He lives in Miami, though. He's only here visiting his dad for the summer,' Nova said, hardly able to keep the disappointment out of her voice.

'Ah hah,' Grandma Rosalind said. 'Well, don't worry, my dear. If it's meant to be it will be, like that Spanish song, eh? Que sera sera!' she laughed, and Nova smiled and shrugged.

'I guess so.'

Her grandma reached over and took her hand, looking at Nova earnestly. 'Uh uh, no guessing. *Know*, my dear. Have faith! Eh heh!' She pulled Nova to jump down from the wall for a cuddle. Then Grandma released her and said, 'Your grandpa and I, God rest him, when we met, it was only a month before he was coming over here to London to study. I was to stay in Salone. But we wrote letters, and a year later – the *minute* he touched back down in Freetown – see how he was down on one knee!'

Nova chuckled, but said, 'Steady on, Grandma, not sure we're quite there yet.'

Her grandma tutted, smiling up at Nova as she still held her granddaughter's hand, resting it on the material of her brightly coloured top, pulled taut by her ample bosom. 'Believe me, it will work out if it is meant to be. Now . . . You 'kin get you gramma a nice cold glass of ginger beer? And pick those cloves out for me, heh?'

Nova smiled and agreed to do so, heading back into the kitchen to fetch her grandma's drink. She struggled to think how Grandma Rosalind's suggestion could be right. How *could* things actually work out with her and Sam? After dropping off the ice-cold ginger beer with her grandma, she realised it was time she was heading to the Brockwell Lido to meet Gemma. Even though the queue on a hot day like today would be madness, Nova was eager to partake in their regular summertime outing to pretend they were on the French Riviera when they were really just by a giant pool in Herne Hill. She even had on the swimsuit Sam had bought her under her clothes.

'I'm off to the lido,' she called to her mum, who had now been joined by her dad in the kitchen. Otis was busily serving out the front, along with Kenny, one of his friends who was getting some extra cash by helping out. 'See you later.'

The burning sun made Nova doubly eager to splash into that pool. She gave Gemma a call as she walked to the lido, and heard lots of chatter on the line as her friend answered.

'Hey, babe!' Gemma said, then called out 'hi' to someone else. 'Sorry, Tiegen and Ruth are ahead of me in the queue, I thought I might try and sneak up there. Are you gonna be here soon? To be honest, I'm sure we'll still be waiting. It's a roadblock here!'

Nova was really glad to be catching up with some of her other mates from school, too. It felt like ages since the start of summer. She popped in her headphones, and the walk was just long enough for her to get three listens in of the song she and Sam had worked on amongst the magical trees at the festival. It still sounded really good, and as she listened, she scrolled through his messages again, smiling down at her phone. She had sent him the recording, and he'd said they should record it properly. She had agreed to take the dinner shift in the restaurant the next day, but on Friday she and Sam had organised a date to *finally* hang out in London.

But for now, she jogged across the road to where the queue was snaking into the car park next to the lido. She saw Gemma waving frantically, and Nova tried to make herself invisible as she slipped in near the front of the queue with her friends, trying to ignore the irritation on the faces of the people behind them as Gemma squealed and squeezed Nova into a hug.

'Subtle, hon,' Nova said jokingly, pulling an apologetic face at the people she'd jumped in front of. She gave Tiegen and Ruth each a hug, and they all cheered along with the five people in front of them as a big group of ten or so left the poolside, freeing up space. A sweating, harangued lifeguard let them all in, and the girls eagerly set up their towels beside the water. Nova took up Gemma's offer to smooth on some of her expensive sun protection cream that smelled like holidays. The four friends stripped off a little self-consciously, before settling back on their towels to soak in the rays.

Nova could only stand it for ten minutes before she had to dive into the cool water, which was heaving with people flirting and splashing. A serious swimmer-type older lady looked at the young people around her with a frown. Nova had no idea why anyone would think doing lane swimming would be possible on a day like today! She balanced her elbows on the side of the pool as she re-tied her locs to balance higher on her head.

'You guys should get in here!' she told her friends. 'It is *delicious*!'

Gemma scooted to the edge of the water and dangled her lower legs in, leaning back in her bikini to take a few selfies. 'This is as far as I'll go, babe. Chlorine and these crochet locs do not mix.'

Nova flicked water at her, giggling. 'That's why you should bite the bullet and grow the real thing,' she teased, but she suddenly noticed Gemma's face turning serious as she looked past where Nova was floating. Glancing at Tiegen and Ruth, Nova realised they had sour looks on their faces, too.

'Uh, babe . . .' Gemma began, and Nova turned around to see what they were all looking at. Stretching out his – admittedly amazing – abs while he adjusted some goggles, Nathan, in his form-fitting swimming shorts, was preparing to dive in on the other side of the pool. He was mainly posing, and it was clearly having an effect on the young women and a few of the guys around the pool and in the water.

'Fan-tastic,' Nova muttered.

'Yeah.' Gemma lowered her voice. 'Uh, and I kind of meant to tell you . . . Rumour has it he's broken up with Amanda.'

Nova dipped herself under the water for a moment – partly to cool off, partly to avoid Gemma's eyes as she broke that nugget of news.

'OK. Well, good for her, lucky escape, I'd say,' Nova said as she emerged.

Gemma nodded. 'Just ignore him, yeah?'

But that was easier said than done. As her friend spoke, Clive ran up behind Nathan and pushed him into the water. Nate splashed into the pool, swimming away a few strokes and breaking the surface . . . right next to Nova.

'Oh, hey, sorry. Clive being hilarious, as usual,' Nathan said sarcastically, then eyeing Nova's orange swimsuit in the water. 'How's it going?'

Nova pushed down the urge inside her to splash a huge wave of water in his face and swim away. 'Fine,' she said, beginning to turn away towards Gemma and the girls, but she stopped as she felt Nathan's hand on her shoulder.

'Uh, Nova, I've been meaning to drop you a message . . . You know, just to say how sorry I am with how things ended between us.'

Nova clung to the edge of the pool to keep afloat. 'Right,' she said. 'And this wouldn't have anything to do with you breaking up with the girl you broke up with me for?' She studied him, realising something. '*Oh*. She broke up with *you*, didn't she?' Nova failed to stifle a slight smile. 'Hurts, doesn't it?'

Nathan kicked his strong legs to tread water. 'I guess it kind of made me come to my senses about—'

Nova was about to interject when she heard Gemma's voice, and her shadow looming over them in the water. 'Er, let me stop you there, *Nathan*.' She managed to make his name sound like a swear word. 'My girl here has very much moved on, with a very-much-hotter American man. So maybe swim along, eh?'

Nova cringed, but only a little – the look on Nate's face at this information was worth the embarrassment of the ripple of whispers around them as the gossip of this encounter spread. Whatever. Gemma was right! She had moved on, and seeing Nate today had cemented that.

'You *are* still with your Yank hottie, right?' Gemma said under her breath as Nova pulled herself out of the pool to flop back on to her towel.

'Definitely,' Nova said with a sigh, then told Gemma, Ruth and Tiegen all about WildArts, their little hiccup, and the ridiculously romantic night under the trees.

'Wow,' Ruth breathed, reaching for Tiegen's hand and looking at her dreamily. Nova's eyes widened at the two of them, and then she pointed a finger between them.

'Wait . . . are you two . . . ?'

Tiegen grinned. 'Yup!'

'Aaargh, that's amazing!' Nova exclaimed, reaching over to hug them both.

'Ooh, so much gossip today!' Gemma exclaimed, squeezing their friends' hands and then pushing her sunglasses on to her head. 'I am *living* for this! You two are so perfect for each other!'

Nova turned to her best mate. 'Thanks for intervening with Nate there, Gem.'

'No worries,' Gemma said, situating her sunglasses back over her eyes. 'He's an idiot, and he needed to be told.'

Nova sat cross-legged, facing her friends. 'Yeah, definitely.' She sighed again. 'I'm just a bit worried about what will happen when Sam goes back to the States.'

Gemma propped herself on to her elbows as she lay back, her brown stomach taut with muscles Nova had to admit she envied. 'Babe, Tim Berners-Lee did not invent the Worldwide Web for this kind of attitude! You can keep in touch, and he might fly over to visit his dad. You could see if you can do a gap year, too. Oooh, or even do uni in Florida . . . !'

Nova nodded. 'I suppose so. It's just even being apart for a few days feels rubbish, so what's it going to be like spending months apart? Who knows what could happen while he's over there with all those Miami dream girls.'

'Hello, you are crushing *hard* on Señor Rodriguez, babe!' Gemma said, raising an eyebrow, but then her expression softened. 'He's not Nate, Nov,' her friend affirmed. 'He's a sweetheart. And from what I saw, he's definitely smitten with you, too. Have faith!'

'That's what my grandma said, too.'

Gemma rolled on to her stomach, gesturing wide with her hands. 'And Grandma Rosalind never lies. Trust it, hon. Trust *him*.'

Nova really wanted to believe all the positive thoughts were true, but she couldn't shake the feeling, deep down, that Sam was holding something back from her. Maybe she'd find out more when they finally met up again. Friday couldn't come soon enough!

CHAPTER 22

Nova felt fluttering butterflies in her stomach as she changed on to the Northern Line at Stockwell for the journey up to Camden Town. She had been keen to try and scope out where Sam and his dad were living, but once again he was characteristically vague about it. What he had said was that he wanted to visit some of Nova's favourite places in London, and she couldn't resist suggesting Camden. There were a few things about the area that she knew he'd love. She just made sure they were heading there early, before the crowds of tourists made it too hellish.

As she exited the tube station a while later, Nova looked around and spotted Sam leaning against a wall nearby with a backpack and headphones on, bopping unselfconsciously to what he was listening to. When he saw Nova he straightened, moving his Conversed foot from the wall to the ground and pushing his hair back in that familiar, ridiculously cute way he did. His skin glowed brown in the summer sun, and Nova was surprised to see him in a short-sleeved button down bowling shirt. Even though it was untucked over his jeans, it gave him a slightly more formal look, and she was very glad she'd followed Gemma's advice to throw on 'something cute'. She tugged at her yellow, strappy sundress as she made her way over to Sam, who beamed widely.

'You, Ms Clarke, are a sight for sore eyes. I just saw a guy with a ton of facial piercings puke on the ground. He was holding one of those signs pointing to a tattoo parlour, and after he threw up he carried on with his sign-holding like it was no biggie!' Sam said, his face momentarily folding into a grimace.

'Well, you've got to admire his dedication to his job,' Nova said, laughing. 'Welcome to Camden!'

Sam pulled her into a hug, kissing her head and then moving down her cheek until his lips found her mouth. 'I'm so freaking glad just to be wherever you are,' he said, his voice that soul-melting low rumble, and Nova felt her face heat. He straightened up a bit. 'Though I've got to say, I thought you Londoners were a little more territorial about your north-south river divide, no? At least according to my pop.'

Nova stood back, tensing defensively even as she smiled up at Sam. 'Hey, hey, I'm south 'til I die,' she said. 'But there are one or two things around here that get me nostalgic. Gem used to bring me up here all the time when we first met, because her parents had only just moved down to Clapham and she was constantly missing this area. There are some pretty cool things we're going to check out. Trust me, I've got it all planned.'

Sam gestured in front of them. 'Sounds dope.

I'm ready! *Vámonos!*'

Nova loved the feeling of Sam slinging his arm around her shoulders, and she steered him across the road and only a short walk from the tube. She gestured up at the white façade of the first place she wanted to take him, grinning as he looked up at the blue neon wording on the front of the building: *London's Famous Jazz Venue*. The Jazz Café had been an iconic music venue for years, hosting some of Nova's all-time favourite artists.

'Wow, seriously? I love it already,' Sam said, squeezing her in closer to him. Music was already spilling out on to the street, and a big, slightly bored-looking security guard stood outside.

'I love this venue,' Nova said eagerly. 'My dad knows the owner coz he used to play here sometimes, so I've been lucky to sneak into some shows despite not being eighteen. Usually they're only open at night, but there's a daytime showcase for up-and-coming artists today, all ages.' She produced two tickets with a flourish. 'Shall we?'

'Heck yeah!'

They headed inside, blinking as they entered the moody, dark space with its little stage, and the balcony hanging over the dance floor. A small jazz ensemble was already up on the stage. A girl with elaborate blonde-brown braids piled up on her head was soloing incredibly on her saxophone, backed by a young guy with a wispy beard on piano and a smiling, bald-headed guy playing the double-bass, the stage lights glowing off his dark skin. Mesmerised by the music, Sam and Nova let off whoops and claps as the group finished their set.

Sam bought some soft drinks, and they settled in a little booth at the back to listen to a nervous but talented guy with an old-school high-top fade singing a couple of neo-soul ballads. The crowd were encouraging, but Nova could sympathise with his apparent stage fright.

'This is so cool,' Sam said during the interval in bands. He edged closer to her in the booth, his arm around her once more as he gave her a gentle kiss. Nova returned it, loving the feel of his hair entwining around her fingers as she pulled him closer. Eventually, she broke away, smiling.

'We should probably head off in a minute, actually. I've got some other stuff to show you, and it gets pretty crowded around here, so it would be good to avoid being swept up in a tsunami of dawdling visitors . . .'

Sam elbowed her jokingly. 'Hey, tourists have the right to dawdle.' He eyed her. 'I myself am very much enjoying the London experience so far. I need to take it all in while I can.'

Nova looked down, away from his gaze, and began to slide out of the booth. She didn't want them to have to start talking about what would happen when Sam had to head back to the States yet. Instead, she grabbed his hand and they headed up the bustling high street, with its vendors spilling on to the pavement. Eventually, she led Sam into Camden Stables market. Inevitably, there was a large crowd around their destination, but Nova felt a well of emotion as she pulled Sam towards the bronze statue of her idol.

'Amy,' she breathed, and looked up at Sam. The statue of Amy Winehouse with her classic beehive and hand-on-hip pose was swathed with flowers at her feet.

'It's the anniversary . . . ?' Sam asked, and Nova nodded. It still hardly seemed real that such an incredibly talented woman had died so tragically young. Eventually they were able to get close enough to the monument to really look, and noticed that people had tied bracelets to Amy's arms. Nova was touched as she saw Sam remove the little black string bracelet he had on, and reach out to tie it on to the statue.

He looked down at Nova with a sad smile, and quietly said, 'I . . . sometimes I think about my dad, about how he struggled with his alcoholism? Even though I was just a kid, I could feel it, you know? How tough it was for him, as well as how it affected all of us. But being over here with him for these last few weeks, I do think he's been trying really hard to stay sober.' He sighed, looking back at the statue. 'It sucks that some people don't get to overcome it.'

Nova took Sam's hand, weaving her fingers in between his as they walked slowly away. 'I'm so glad you're getting a chance to reconnect with your dad,' Nova said, then ventured, 'I'd really like to meet him.'

Sam's pace quickened, even though he didn't know where Nova planned to take them next. He was quiet, as though he was avoiding what she'd said, and began to browse a stall of music-related T-shirts. Holding one up, he said, 'Huh, this is pretty cool . . .'

'Sam . . .' Nova began, feeling her brows knit. But she didn't want to ruin things by asking some of the questions that were on the tip of her tongue. Was Sam ashamed of her or something? She hated to even think it, but would his dad have a problem with his son dating a black girl? It just seemed odd that he got so evasive whenever she tried to talk about where they lived, or meeting his dad. Or maybe there was something else holding Sam back? She remembered how vulnerable she had felt introducing her school friends to her little flat in Brixton. Maybe Sam was self-conscious about his dad's living situation for some reason? She hated to think he'd imagine her being judgemental. But for now she decided to leave it alone.

'Let's get going, eh?' she said.

They headed out of the market and up the street, and Nova felt a sense of relief as they began to leave the crowds of tourists behind. She pointed out another legendary music venue as they headed past it – the Roundhouse, a performing arts space that had apparently held one of the only concerts the Doors played in the UK with Jim Morrison. She wasn't all that familiar with their music, but Sam, who liked a bit of old-school rock, suggested to her which of their songs to check out. The shops and cafés got increasingly fancy as they headed away from the centre of Camden, but Nova had a particular favourite sandwich shop that she and Gemma had made one of their regular haunts when Nova used to come there with her. She led Sam inside the welcoming space, but shook her head when he began to sit down at one of the little tables.

'Nope. We're getting some bits for a picnic,' she said, ordering some sandwiches and a couple of the delicious cupcakes. 'My treat!'

She paid, and the lady behind the counter bagged up their food. Nova could sense the posh girls sitting at a wrought iron table outside were checking Sam out – and who could blame them – but Sam ignored their appreciative glances. His arm was firmly around her shoulders again, kissing her temple as they walked away. Nova loved how he seemed so comfortable in showing the world they were together, and again her heart ached for the day they might have to part.

'OK, here we go!' Nova said, heading through the gates into the vast green expanse of Primrose Hill. It was glorious in the bright summer sunshine. She spun around, then jogged up the inclining path towards a big chestnut tree. Pulling a throw out of her backpack, Nova laid it on the ground for her and Sam to sit on.

'Wow, this is perfect,' he said, stretching out to lie on his side, facing Nova. She took the opportunity to really look at him as he closed his eyes and turned his face towards the sun for a moment.

He is, truly, stunning! Nova thought, barely believing that this was actually her boyfriend! Sam opened his eyes, grinning slowly as he caught her looking at him. Nova blushed, and quickly set about unpacking the sandwiches. They ate contentedly, and then Sam reached up to wipe a little of the buttercream frosting Nova had in the corner of her mouth from her cake. When they were done eating, they lay next to each other, like they had at WildArts. Sam settled his backpack under their heads for a pillow, and they once again looked up through the tree branches. He pulled Nova close to him.

'You know, I've been thinking . . .' he began, and Nova tensed, in spite of how wonderful she felt in his arms.

'Yeah?' Nova said. She felt Sam stir, and she sat up a little. He sat up too, reaching behind him to

315

pick up a blade of grass, which he fiddled with as he spoke.

'I've been thinking . . . Maybe I could come here to finish up with high school. Uh, sixth form, I guess you call it here?'

Nova's eyes widened. 'Really? Like, seriously?'

Sam nodded, still playing with the grass. 'I mean, it would be tough to leave my mom and Teo, is the thing. But it's been kind of cool spending time with my dad, and . . .' He looked at her. 'Honestly? Every time I think about heading back home without you being there, I feel really messed up, Nova. I want to spend way more time with you than just a summer.'

Nova was almost speechless as he reached out and took her hand, his lips quirking a bit. 'In case you hadn't noticed, I'm super into you.' He kissed her knuckles, and Nova felt a swoop in her stomach.

'It would be amazing if you could stay,' she said quietly. 'That's been on my mind a lot, too.'

Sam sighed and lay on his back again. 'I guess we'll have to see what happens . . .'

It was only the sound of her phone ringing that made Nova realise she'd drifted off to sleep in the warm sunshine. She felt Sam move, and lifted her cheek from where it had made its way to his chest. He looked down at her with an amused expression.

'I wasn't snoring, was I?' she asked, quickly checking her mouth for drool.

'Only in, like, the most adorable way,' Sam said. 'I mean, if a motorbike is adorable.' She sat up, jabbing him jokingly in the ribs. 'OK, OK, I'm kidding,' he said, laughing.

Nova quickly picked up her phone, returning a missed call from her mum. It was heading towards five in the evening, and it would take her an hour or so to get back to Brixton. Deana wanted Nova to pick up a watch she'd left at the repair place on her way home before it closed.

'I've got to head back,' she told Sam as she finished the quick call.

Sam's disappointed expression mirrored her

own feelings. But then his face brightened. 'You know what? I've been missing out on my fix of Eats & Beats grub. How would you feel about me heading down with you to get some dinner? I'd love to see the restaurant, and your folks.'

For a moment she felt like pulling Sam up on the fact that he'd met her whole family, but was still being evasive about his dad, but she dismissed it. Getting to extend their date sounded good to her.

'I'd feel pretty good about it,' she said, teasingly. They headed for the tube station, and Nova relished snuggling up to Sam on their journey. If he did stay in the UK . . . ? She almost didn't dare to hope that they could actually have a chance to continue their relationship.

When they emerged out of the tube into the busy chaos of Brixton, Nova watched to see Sam's reaction to the contrast between this area and the fancy environs of Primrose Hill. But he seemed equally at home in both. He scrolled his phone casually as Nova popped into the dilapidated kiosk where she needed to collect her mum's watch. She quickly texted Otis to get him to give their parents a heads-up about Sam coming to the restaurant. She endured the light ribbing her brother gave her in his message back; it was better that he prep their parents than having to go through the embarrassment of Sam turning up unexpectedly!

But nevertheless, as Nova tentatively led Sam down the road towards the restaurant, she was glad to see that it was bustling with people again, so there wasn't quite as much opportunity for her mum and dad to give Sam the third degree. She brought him through to the kitchen to say hello quickly.

'Ah, Sam my man, good to see you, good to see you,' her dad said effusively, giving Sam a pat on the back. Her mum waved from where she was sweating over a vast frying pan of sliced plantain.

'Hello, dear,' she said, grinning broadly at Nova, who quickly served up two plates of her

 319

dad's curry goat for her and Sam, handing him one and leading him back outside to one of the tables that had been freed up on the pavement. They tucked in, and Sam did an exaggerated chef's kiss as he took his first forkfuls of the food.

'I definitely get why you guys won that award,' he said, chewing enthusiastically. Nova heard someone clear their throat, and turned to see her brother holding two ice-cold pineapple drinks.

'Thought you two might need these,' he said, though his eyes rested firmly just on Sam. He set the drinks down then reached a hand out to shake Sam's hand. 'I'm Otis. Nova's brother,' he said, and she could see he was being rather firm with his greeting. Sam nodded, barely wincing at Otis' tight grip, which made Nova smile.

'Hey, man, really good to meet you properly. Sam.'

Otis folded his arms, regarding Sam. 'Yeah, she's been talking about you a fair bit. But you're off back to the States soon. Miami, right?'

Sam pointed to the sports vest Otis was wearing.

'Yeah – you a LeBron fan?' he asked. 'I miss him playing for the Heat!'

Otis looked down at his top, and when he looked back up he was wearing an expression that Nova knew meant he was giving Sam the benefit of the doubt, at least. He nodded. 'You must get to see the Lakers play every now and then, right?'

Sam crunched up his face. 'Don't rub it in, man. But things have really been looking up for Miami this season . . .'

Nova tuned out as they began to discuss basketball for a fraction longer than she was willing to tolerate, and she popped open the can of fizzy drink pointedly.

'Oh, my bad, beautiful,' Sam said, earning a raised eyebrow from Otis.

'I suppose I'll leave you to it, seeing as this one has weaselled her way out of a shift tonight,' he said, winking at his sister. 'Good to meet you, mate.'

The happy, smug feeling Nova had must have shown on her face, because Sam asked, 'What?'

She pushed her plate away and rested her hand on her chin contentedly as she looked at Sam. 'Nothing, it's just nice that you've fully won my family over.' She paused, sipping her drink, and drew a breath. 'They weren't so keen on Nate.'

Sam's face turned a little stonier. 'Nate – the ex?'

Nova nodded. 'I suppose I was wasting my time on him,' she said softly, still looking at Sam. 'Or biding my time without knowing it, until the right boy came along.'

Sam's eyes filled with emotions Nova wasn't sure she was ready for. She picked up her empty plate and put it on top of Sam's, standing up from the table. 'Better clear this stuff away,' she said.

'Sure,' Sam said, as though he knew she might need a moment. 'I'll help.' He slung his backpack on to one shoulder and followed after her.

Back in the kitchen, her dad was serenading her mum with an Al Green song, pretending his serving spoon was a microphone. As ever, his vocals were strong and melodic, and Sam grinned as he saw

322

the scene unfold – and, no doubt, the mortified look on Nova's face.

'Guys . . .' she began, but soon Sam was putting his bag down in the corner and enthusiastically harmonising with her dad. She covered her face with her hand, laughing beneath it. Her dad spun her around into Sam's arms, and he danced with her as they sang, her mum even joining in for a second before calling Otis to collect an order through the hatch. The kitchen filled with laughter, but eventually they calmed down. Hector clapped Sam on the shoulder.

'You've got a great voice, man,' her dad said. 'Nova mentioned you're a musician?'

'And you are too, right?' Sam asked. Her dad brushed it off, and Nova caught Sam's eye.

'Here and there, here and there,' her dad said. 'I gave up on the bigger dream a while ago. But your father is in the industry too, my girl says? Is that right? What are his thoughts on this music thing?'

Nova watched Sam closely at this, but he scratched the back of his neck and shrugged. 'I guess he'd agree that it's a tough business.' He looked at Nova. 'But I really want to try and pursue it, see where I can get with it.' Sam smiled, but she was glad he left it at that, and didn't try to persuade her dad that she should be focussing on her music, too.

Eventually it was time for Sam to head home. He pulled out a hoodie from his bag as the cooler evening drew in, and they headed out of the restaurant. As the streetlights illuminated overhead, she walked him slowly to the end of the street, holding hands.

'Get home safely, yeah?' she said. 'Message me when you get in.'

'Are you saying these mean London streets might eat a naïve Florida boy up?' He grinned at her as she pursed her lips. 'I promise.' He pecked her mouth, and she relaxed it enough for him to kiss her properly.

'Oh, I meant to ask – is your dad working at CityFest?' Nova had thought maybe her parents would give up their slot at the one-day London festival, but they had decided to go anyway, seeing as it was local.

Sam avoided her eye as he shook his head. 'That's next weekend, right? Uh, there's this thing I said I'd turn up for with my dad and his new girlfriend, so I won't make it to that one.'

Nova nodded, trying not to feel weird that once again, evasive-Sam had appeared. 'OK, no worries,' she said, disappointed. 'But I'll see you during the week, yeah?'

He leaned down to press his forehead to hers. 'Just try to keep me away,' he whispered, and then kissed her goodbye.

Nova drifted back towards the café, and Otis mimicked her soppy grin as she came back inside. 'Practically got love-hearts floating out of your eyes,' he said, and she picked up a napkin to throw at him.

'Ah, Nova,' her mum said, wiping her hands on her apron then pulling out a piece of paper from where it was tucked under her arm. 'I think your little friend dropped this?'

'My little friend?' Nova said, chuckling as she took the piece of paper. It was a letter, with no envelope, but a distinctive letterhead. 'Err, thanks Mum.' Nova headed upstairs, looking at the piece of paper. *London College of Music*? She knew she shouldn't pry, but the letter was clearly inviting Sam for an audition! Maybe he was more serious than she thought about staying in the UK? Her heart fluttered, but she was equally curious when she saw the address the letter was sent to.

'Holland Park?' she mused out loud. She flopped on to her bed upstairs and pulled up the map app on her phone. She knew the area was in West London somewhere, and that it was a fancy part of town. Was that really where Sam's dad lived? Then again, she knew that in London you could have mansions on one street then turn a corner to a housing estate on the next. From the map location that came up, she had a strange feeling that Sam's dad was more in the former than the latter, though. 'Weird,' she whispered.

But for now, she didn't want anything to

dampen the excited feeling she had thinking about the possibility of Sam staying in London – and in her life – for more perfect days like the one she'd just shared with him.

CHAPTER 23

Nova clutched Gemma's hand tightly as they both bounced up and down, singing at the top of their lungs along with everybody else in the crowd to the final chorus of 'I'm Every Woman'. Admittedly, most of the people around them were significantly older, but Nova could hardly believe that *actual* Chaka Khan was on stage at CityFest! She was a legend, and Nova remembered her mum and dad playing her music and dancing around the living room when she was a kid. She had loved Chaka's voice ever since, and was thrilled that she'd spent enough energy turning Gemma on to the singer that she was equally excited to go and see her performance, too!

'You have been a beautiful audience!' Chaka said, waving as she exited the stage, her huge, signature reddish-purple wig seeming to float around her head.

'Wow!' Gemma said, still clapping.

'I know, right?'

Nova's mind drifted unintentionally over to Sam as she and Gemma made their way back to the food truck. She had messaged him the day before, saying how excited she was about seeing Chaka Khan perform at CityLit festival, and of course he'd secured major brownie points by saying he loved her music, too, and how jealous he was. Nova had really wanted to ask him about the audition at the college – or even wish Sam luck with it – but seeing as he hadn't told her about it, she felt weird mentioning it. The whole thing made her uneasy, but she pushed it to the back of her mind again for now. Even though CityFest was only a day-long affair, Nova's family arrived early with the truck, and it had been chock-a-block with customers ever since. Nova had agreed to take over from Otis that afternoon so he could check out one of his favourite rappers performing on the headline stage.

'Go on then,' Nova said to Otis, making her way up the back steps and into the food truck. 'Go get your head-nod on!'

Otis grinned. 'Nice one, sis.' His smile turned towards Gemma, who was lingering just out the back, and Nova eyed them both closely. 'Hey, Gem.' Otis' greeting sounded almost shy, and Nova actually thought it was kind of sweet.

Taking a breath, she said slyly, 'Gem, weren't you were saying how much you were getting into J. Cole the other day? Ots, you wouldn't mind her tagging along to watch him with you, would you?' She turned to her friend. 'I feel bad I have to abandon you for this shift, babe . . .'

Gemma looked not even a little bit sad about it, especially with Otis' enthusiastic nodding.

'Course!' he said, and Nova smiled as she

watched her brother and her best friend head away from the truck in the overcast afternoon warmth. She sighed a little, putting on her Eats & Beats apron, but then had a thought. This might be one of the last shifts she'd have to do in the truck! She almost felt nostalgic about it, but as the afternoon wore on she began thinking that wrapping things up at the food truck would be no bad thing. That was until a ripple of people started turning and pointing their phone cameras, staring at someone coming towards the truck.

'Is that . . . ?' she began, turning to her mum, who was also squinting out at the crowd gathering in front of Eats & Beats. It was hard to see clearly, because there was a man-mountain holding an umbrella over a diminutive figure. But as they got closer, Nova definitely recognised that distinctive hair. 'Oh. My. *Gosh*. It is!'

'Uh, M-Ms Khan!' Nova's mum stuttered as the queue parted for the beautiful singer and her bodyguard.

'Hey, how's it going?' Chaka said with her

broad, red-lipped smile, while Nova did an impression of her childhood pet goldfish, opening and closing her mouth. Her dad was going to seriously regret having picked this moment to go and fetch more ice! Nova could barely focus as she heard the singer explaining how she liked to try out different food, and that her 'good friend Clay Cooper' had said such wonderful things about Eats & Beats!

'When I saw you guys on the list of vendors, I had to come check things out for myself,' she said. Nova and her mum practically fell over themselves recommending dishes and putting together an order for her and her entourage. When they'd bagged everything up, Nova plucked up her courage to ask for a picture.

'Sure, honey!'

Nova rushed out of the truck with her phone. She posed, trying not to fangirl too hard. Chaka eventually headed away, with her minder carrying the recycled paper bags filled with food, and Nova sent Sam the photographic evidence of the epic turn of events.

Actually cannot believe this just happened! she wrote, grinning. She headed back into the truck, and Nova and her mum gripped hands and squealed simultaneously.

'What did I miss?' Nova's dad said, arriving with a bag of ice in each hand.

Deana explained, and she and Nova pulled sympathetic-but-amused expressions as Hector took the news in. Nova's mum consoled him by saying how many portions of his curry goat Chaka had ordered!

As the festival began to wind down, Nova's mum suggested that she start packing up some stuff into Otis' car boot, because the traffic out of the site was bound to be a nightmare. But as Nova carried a spare box of containers over to where her brother's car was parked, she slowed to a stop, almost dropping it. She saw Otis standing next to his precious vehicle – *kissing Gemma!*

'Whoa!' Nova whispered to herself, quickly doing an about-turn to give them some privacy.

She was surprised at just how happy she felt for Gemma and Otis, even if it was kind of gross to think about, too. She decided it was best to lurk behind one of the catering tents until she was sure the coast was clear, and her own romantic feelings swelled as she felt her phone ringing and saw Sam's name on the screen.

'Was that Chaka Khan, for real?' he asked as soon as she answered. Nova laughed.

'Yep!' she said, explaining the whole surreal experience to Sam. 'Really wish you'd been here!' she finished, hoping he might take the opportunity to come clean with her about the audition. She waited, but instead heard what sounded like live music striking up in the background on his end of the call. 'Are you at home?' she asked, frowning.

'Uh . . . No, I'm at a thing, like I told you. Something my pops dragged me to,' Sam said, once again frustratingly vague.

Nova sighed hard. 'Right,' she said, and the sound on the other end of the line grew more faint, as though Sam had moved somewhere quieter.

'Yeah, it's lame,' Sam said. 'I'd much rather be hanging out with you and Chaka.'

But this time, Nova didn't want to let him charm his way out of her question marks over his behaviour. 'Yeah,' she said pointedly. 'Well, maybe I could come by yours tomorrow, and we can hang out?'

She knew he'd bat this idea away almost as soon as the words left her lips. 'Sure . . .' he began. 'Or maybe we can hook up somewhere and go to the movies? Or I could take you to go get some foo—'

'Sam,' Nova said, cutting him off. 'You're not . . . You're not ashamed of me, are you?'

The pause and sharp exhale she now heard through her earpiece at least gave her some comfort. 'Nova! Of course I'm not ashamed of you. Are you kidding me? I'm proud— I'm frankly *amazed* you even entertain the idea of me being your guy. I . . . Things are just a little complex with my dad and whatnot. And more than anything, I don't want any of that stuff to get in

335

the way of us.'

Nova wasn't sure how to respond to that, so just said, 'OK. I just wanted to be sure.' She looked up, spotting Otis and Gemma walking away hand in hand. 'Listen, I'd better go. I'll give you a call in a bit and we can arrange something for tomorrow, yeah?'

'Absolutely,' Sam said, still sounding a bit shaken. 'Nova, I'm real sorry I couldn't be there today. I promise you, I'm figuring things out.'

'Cool,' she replied softly. 'I'll speak to you later, OK?'

As she hung up, she wished she had just asked him outright about the audition, but something told her it was best to let Sam do things on his own terms for now.

An hour later, and everything was packed up ready for Nova's parents to drive the truck back to the garage – a friend of theirs had sorted them out with a deal to store it near the restaurant when they weren't using it. Nova had half-expected Gemma to change the plans they had to head back to her house in Clapham and hang out that evening, given what had clearly happened with Otis. But instead, she watched Gemma and her brother coyly saying goodbye to one another, exchanging secret smiles that made Nova jealous all over again that Sam wasn't there.

They said bye to her parents, and Otis headed off to the pub with a couple of his mates. Gemma linked arms with Nova as they walked to the pick-up spot to wait for the cab she had called. Nova had suggested the bus would be fine, but Gemma had already pulled out her phone to get on the app.

'My treat, hon.'

While they waited, Nova drew a breath to ask Gemma about Otis at the very same time as her friend did the same.

'So . . .' they both began simultaneously, then burst into giggles.

Nova grinned. 'Feel like there's something you might want to tell me about you and Ots?'

Gemma nodded enthusiastically. 'Oh, babes, I hope you won't find it weird. But, like, oh my gosh! Me and your brother! He's ridiculously dreamy and we were talking loads, and then we were watching J. Cole perform, and then he was holding my hand, and then we kissed . . .'

Nova couldn't help screwing her face up into a grimace even as she smiled. 'Yeah, I feel like I'll need a bit less in the way of detail, hon,' she said with a laugh. 'But that's amazing! I'm honestly really happy for you guys.' She squeezed Gemma's arm harder, before they broke apart as the cab arrived and they got into the back, confirming Gemma's name and address.

Nova turned to her friend. 'So I spoke to Sam . . .'

'Yeah? Everything cool?'

She wasn't sure how to answer her friend's question. 'I think so? I mean, he's been a bit evasive lately. And I found a letter of his about an audition for a music college here in London . . .'

Gemma's eyebrows shot towards her hairline. 'No way! Like, he might be staying here?'

Nova half-shrugged, half-nodded. 'Thing is, he hasn't told me about it directly. Not to mention that every time I try to suggest coming to visit him, he's all weird about it.'

'Hmm,' Gemma said, seeming just as puzzled about Sam's behaviour as Nova was – but as usual, she tried to see the bright side. 'I'm sure there's a good reason for all of it, though, hon. Maybe he wanted it to be a surprise?'

'Maybe.'

They fell silent for a while, and Gemma glanced back at her phone. 'Huh,' she said, and Nova turned to her again.

'What?'

Gemma was staring at her screen, moving the phone closer to her face as though she needed to inspect it more closely. 'Err . . . this is bizarre.'

Nova reached over and gently pulled the phone out of her friend's hands to see what she was staring at. On the screen, she saw an image that was definitely bizarre, to say the least. She fell silent, still gazing at it, and she only vaguely heard Gemma ask, 'That's . . . That's Sam, isn't it?'

Nova felt like she was hallucinating. But sure enough, on Sadie Varma's Instagram feed, there was a picture of Sadie with her arms draped around two men – Clay Cooper, with his arm around her waist, smiling at her. The other guy was looking unimpressed with Sadie's hand on his shoulder. The caption beneath the post said something about 'my man @ClayCooper and his gorgeous son, Yosemite, at tonight's epic launch of *Sadie Varma Sparkle*'.

'Yeah,' she whispered. Her voice sounded alien. She could hardly compute it, but suddenly things started to make sense. 'Sam . . . is Clay Cooper's son.'

CHAPTER 24

Nova listened to Gemma snoring softly on her luxurious double bed. She lay awake on the sofa bed across the room, and could see the sun beginning to rise through a crack in the curtains. They had stayed up extra late after Nova's parents had OKed her sleeping over at her best friend's house. Of course, Nova hadn't elaborated to them on the events that had unfolded in the cab ride back to Gemma's. It still all felt so surreal, and she hadn't yet had the strength to confront Sam about what she had seen on Sadie Varma's social media feed.

Or not Sam. 'Yosemite'. Nova sighed, fighting off more tears. She had ignored the call and texts from Sam last night, light-heartedly trying to arrange for them to meet up tomorrow – or today, she supposed. But she'd lain awake most of the night, attempting to reconcile the amazing relationship she thought she had been forming with him, and the fact he'd been lying to her this whole time. Nova felt so stupid. Having warned herself off a relationship this summer after everything that had happened with Nate, she almost felt like she'd been made an even *bigger* fool of with Sam.

He was, quite literally, not the person she thought he was.

Gemma had suggested that Nova just forget about Sam, and chalk it up to experience. But thinking about it now, Nova couldn't let it lie. She had to confront him. As she watched the sky begin to brighten, she decided that she was going to go and see him that very morning, and attempt to get some explanation face to face.

Waiting for it to be a more sensible time of day, she spent an hour staring at the Instagram feed of the boy she'd thought was Sam Rodriguez, trying not to cry, but also feeling angry for having been taken advantage of. Eventually, she got up and showered in Gemma's en-suite bathroom before getting dressed, hardly thinking about her make-up-free face and her eyes still red from tears and lack of sleep.

'Babe, where are you going?' Gemma said croakily as Nova emerged into the bedroom again and began to pack up her stuff.

'I have to speak to him,' Nova said determinedly, and Gemma sat up in bed quickly.

'OK, I can come with you—' Gemma began, but Nova cut her off.

'It's fine, Gem. Thank you. This is something I think I need to do by myself.'

She reached over to hug her friend goodbye, promising to let her know how things went with Sam, and when she got home. Then Nova headed out of her friend's house, walking to the tube station to make her way over to Holland Park. Nerves began to skitter around in her stomach as she changed on to the Central line and neared her stop. Pulling out her phone and checking the way to the address on the letter Sam had dropped, Nova momentarily wondered if this was a completely crazy thing to do. What if it wasn't even his dad's real address? What if Sam had lied about it for his application? But she'd committed to her plan now, and so using her maps app she began to navigate her way to the address. As she walked through the streets lined with huge houses, it seemed increasingly likely that this was the kind of place that a multi-millionaire rock star would live. A few minutes later, she found herself outside a house that was set back slightly from the road, with a huge, sleek black wooden gate across the entrance. Over the top of the gate, Nova could see a massive, modern-looking house with grey concrete walls and big windows.

Swallowing, she walked up to the panel at the side of the gate, and pressed the bell. There was a slight crackling noise, and then a woman's voice said, 'Yes?'

'Uh . . . I'm . . . Is Sam—' Nova began, then cleared her throat. 'Sorry, I mean, I'm here to see Yosemite.' She drew a breath. 'I'm a friend of his. Is he in?' She felt ridiculous, but stood her ground, waiting.

'Yosemite?' the woman said, but then she heard voices on the other end of the intercom – she thought she heard Sam, and felt another zip of nerves and anger through her body. 'Who is it, please?' the woman asked into the speaker again, and Nova thought she detected a faintly Eastern European accent.

'My name is Nova Clarke.' She tried to sound confident, letting her anger fuel her. There was some more crackling on the line, then a low buzz, and the black gate began to slide open. Nova held her breath, feeling sweat pooling under her arms. She peered into the space that was slowly revealed, and saw a driveway covered in white pebbles, with a Range Rover parked in it, and a green, manicured garden area off to the right. There were a few wide steps leading up to the big, glass front door of the house, which was now opening. Nova squinted as the morning sunlight reflected off it, blinking as she saw Sam standing in the doorway. His feet were bare, and he was wearing loose knitted black shorts and a white T-shirt. He was staring at Nova as though she was painted blue, such was the obvious shock on his face – but as always, he also somehow looked completely gorgeous.

'N-Nova? What . . .? How did you . . .?'

She took a few steps towards him through the gate, which then began to slide closed again – as Nova looked over her shoulder hearing it rumble behind her, she saw a couple of kids craning their necks to see into the compound. Turning back to Sam, she held out the letter.

'You dropped this at the restaurant the other day,' she began, and he padded down the steps to meet her, taking it from her hands and staring down at it. He didn't speak, so she added, 'I suppose I was sort of hoping you'd tell me about the audition yourself, but . . .' Sam looked up at her, and she had a sense that his confusion was beginning to mingle with worry as his forehead wrinkled. 'But that's not the only thing you were keeping from me, clearly.'

She looked up as a middle-aged blonde lady appeared behind Sam in the doorway, looking curious, and holding what looked like a dusting cloth.

'Everything OK, Yosemite?' Nova recognised her voice as the lady on the intercom, and assumed she was some kind of housekeeper. He really did live in a completely different world.

Sam seemed to tense at the woman calling him that. 'It's fine, Greta,' he said quickly. 'Thanks. I'll just be a minute.' The woman eyed Nova a moment longer before heading back inside.

'Yeah, wouldn't want to keep you, *Yosemite*,' Nova said, failing to conceal the anger in her voice.

'Nova . . .' he began, wincing as he stepped on to the gravel, trying to touch her arm. She took a step back. 'I can explain.'

Nova folded her arms in front of her, as though they could protect her from the overwhelming hurt she felt. 'I doubt it. You lied to me, Sa— I mean, I didn't even know your real *name*!' She shook her head, feeling tears threaten again. 'I'm such an idiot.'

'Nova, no . . . Please, listen to me, OK? Samuel's my middle name. I go by it back home, and I use my mom's last name, so that I don't have to deal with all the stuff that comes with people knowing my dad is Clay Cooper,' he said, his eyebrows raised earnestly. Nova looked at him, then looked away again, unable to stop him as he stepped over and gently took her shoulders, but not giving him the satisfaction of unfolding her arms or meeting his eye. 'I wanted to wait and see how the audition went before telling you about it specifically – I haven't even told my dad.' He sighed. 'I guess I didn't want him to get his hopes up over it either, since we're only just figuring things out with each other . . .'

'You mean your dad the international rock star,

lead singer of one of the biggest bands on the planet, the guy you let me believe this whole time was a *roadie*?' She shook her shoulders free of Sam's warm hands, tears beginning to spill. 'How could you do this to me? I trusted you!' She swiped at her cheeks.

'Nova, I'm so sorry, but I didn't lie. Everything I told you was true, all my feelings are—'

But Nova held up a hand. 'Please don't,' she choked out. 'I don't want to hear anything more. Just . . . leave me alone, OK?'

Nova looked around desperately to figure out how to leave, and felt a wash of relief as she saw a button to release a smaller side gate to exit. She pushed it, then stepped outside and on to the pavement, breathing hard.

But that relief was soon swamped by a tidal wave of sadness, anger and hurt as she quickly rushed away from the boy she had fallen for, who had broken her heart all over again.

PART V
Berks Beats

CHAPTER 25

'Awright? How come you're up so . . . ? Ah, it's the big day, eh?' Otis said as he stumbled sleepily into the living room and saw Nova sitting at the breakfast counter in their kitchen, half-heartedly eating a bowl of cornflakes. She nodded, feeling her stomach churn. She put her spoon down with a clink and, contrary to her usual ethos that they should clean up after themselves, Deana reached over with a sympathetic smile to clear the bowl away from the other side of the small counter.

'I have every faith that you've smashed it,' she said to Nova, who wasn't so confident. GCSE results day. What if her grades weren't good enough? What if her plans to ignore the music stuff and fall back on being a parent-pleasing environmental scientist were ripped to shreds when she got her results that morning? Maybe the last week and a half had made her too pessimistic, given everything that had happened with Sam. It felt like walking away from him was a confirmation of the idea that dreams were foolish. She'd dreamt of a future with him, and those dreams had been dashed by his lies. She was a hundred per cent sure now that dreaming of becoming a singer-songwriter was equally silly. But if her exam results weren't what she needed either, then where would she be?

Otis came over and playfully tied a couple of her locs in a bow under Nova's chin while she sat impassively. 'Ah, come on, sis. Cheer up!' He headed into their little kitchen to make himself a cup of tea, and Nova caught her mum giving him the 'cut it out' eyes. Her brother was, of course, all loved up with Gemma, so couldn't relate to Nova's enduring heartache. Still, he was right – moping about wasn't going to help. She undid her hair from under her chin, and took a deep breath as she stood up.

'I suppose I'd better go and get ready,' she said as she heard her dad emerge from the bathroom where he'd been taking his customary long morning shower. 'I said I'd meet Gem at nine-thirty so we could grab a coffee before we head to school to get our results.'

'Oh, yeah?' Otis said, suddenly interested. 'Need a lift?'

That did raise a little smile for Nova. 'Nope, loverboy, the bus will be fine. I need Gem all to myself this morning!'

An hour later, Nova waved from her table in the coffee shop as she saw Gemma bustle in, with yet another new hairstyle. Her hair was cropped short now, her curls bleached blonde and stunning against her dark skin.

'Oh, wow, hello, Jada Pinkett Smith?' Nova said, actually managing to smile.

'Hah, as if,' Gemma said, but she stroked the nape of her neck and turned her head to the side to show off her new look. 'Also, loving this,' she said, gesturing at Nova's face, which turned quizzical. 'The smile? Haven't seen one of those on your face for *tiiime*! Ooh, is this for me?'

She sat down and Nova nodded, watching as her friend gratefully drank the cappuccino she'd already purchased for her. 'I've decided to just try and power through the whole misery of stuff with Sam,' Nova told her friend, who held her hand up for a high five, still drinking. Nova slapped Gemma's palm.

'Yes, exactly, babe,' Gemma said, swallowing. 'Later for him.' But there was something about her expression as she glanced towards her phone, which rested on the table next to her mug.

'What?' Nova asked, eyeing Gemma closely.

Gem shook her head. 'You've unfollowed him and all that, yes?'

'Yeah?'

'OK. Good. Good.'

Nova gave her friend an exasperated tut. 'Oh yeah, that's definitely not going to make me wonder what the heck that means!'

Gemma reached over and touched Nova's hand. 'Look, it's nothing, he's just been posting loads of little songs and whatnot that seem to be about you, and messaging me wanting to talk to you, blah blah.'

'Oh.' Nova's resolve was close to breaking anyway, so this was definitely not the news she wanted to hear.

'Listen, today is not about any of that,' Gemma said. 'We're getting our exam results and thinking about our Miami-boy-free futures, right?'

Nova nodded vigorously. 'You're right.' And she meant it – she'd wasted too much time thinking about boys. Today was about her, and she didn't want anything else to get in the way of finding out her *real* future. 'Let's go!'

A big crowd of their classmates were swarming towards the school as she and Gemma arrived, and they greeted Tiegen and Ruth and a few of their other friends nervously. Ms Hartford and another of their teachers, Mr Blake, began distributing the envelopes that contained the students' results.

'Good luck, Ms Clarke – and you, Ms Aidoo,' Mr Blake said, a smile rippling his pale brown moustache.

Nova held out her envelope to Gemma. 'Moment of truth,' she said, and *clinked* her envelope to her friend's as though it were a glass of champagne. She felt her fingers trembling as she tore it open, and her eyes scanned down the list of subjects.

'Oh, OK . . . OK, cool,' Gemma said, studying her results. 'A seven, six eights and . . . Oooh, four nines!' Her eyes flicked up to meet Nova's. 'Nice!'

'Yeah . . .' Nova said distractedly. *Nice?* Those were stellar results!

'Well?' Gemma asked. 'The suspense is killing me, what did you get?'

Nova held her piece of paper up towards her friend. 'I got eight sevens, two eights and . . .'

'A nine!' Gemma exclaimed. 'Nova, that's fantastic!'

Nova stared at the results again. 'Yeah!'

News soon began to filter around all her classmates as to who achieved which marks, and it definitely seemed like Gemma's were among the highest.

'Congratulations, Nova.' She heard a voice behind her and turned around, already knowing who it would be.

Her jaw tightened when she saw her ex and she said a quick, 'Thanks.'

Nate didn't seem like he was planning to move away though. He stood in front of Nova, playing with his envelope. 'So, um, are you lot going to be at Berks Beats, then?' he asked.

Nova pursed her lips. What was it to him? Not that she was sure if she would be able to go to the last festival of the summer yet. Her parents had decided to skip this one, as they'd mentioned, but Nova was hoping to persuade them to let her go with her friends. 'Maybe,' she told Nate, then quickly turned on her heel to find Gemma and their other friends. She knew Nate was likely to be going, as a big group of them were, but it still put a dampener on the whole idea of an actual festival experience without having to work at Eats & Beats.

But once again, Nova told herself that she wasn't going to let any boy ruin the last bit of her summer break.

'So, tell me again?'

Nova sighed into a smile at her mum, whose arms were crossed as she raised both eyebrows at her daughter expectantly.

'I'm going to check in at ten, three and ten. I'm not going to drink – or do anything else. I'm going to stick with Gem and my other mates at all times. I'm going to keep safe and sensible.'

'And no . . . ?'

Nova laughed, but then tried to stifle it. '"No

getting on any lanky boy's shoulders to see over the crowds."'

'Mmm *hmm*,' her mum said emphatically, even as her dad grinned and handed Nova something wrapped in colourful beeswax wrap.

'Here's some rice bread for the trip,' he told Nova, putting an arm around her shoulder and rubbing it. 'What your mother means to say is we're proud of you, girl, and we trust you. But still, check in with us like she say, OK?'

'*Thanks*, Dad,' she said pointedly, and then gave both her parents tight hugs. 'See you later, Ots,' she told her brother, who was shoving some of his stuff into a backpack. He reached out and touched knuckles with her in their customary way.

'Take care of my girl, yeah?'

'Eeugh,' Nova retorted, smiling. 'Don't spend all your time distracting Gem by messaging her, yeah?'

He grinned. 'No promises!'

Nova was secretly quite glad that Otis already saved up to go for a weekend break with two of his mates to Berlin that had been on the cards for ages, so he wasn't coming to the festival. Last thing she needed was him and Gemma making eyes at each other while she nursed her bruised heart! Overall, though, she was feeling better about ignoring all the stuff that had happened with Sam, and just having an amazing time at the festival with her friends.

That was, until she hopped on the coach next to Gemma, and saw her exchanging glances with Tiegen and Ruth as they sat in the seats across the aisle.

'Err, have you heard about Avant-Garde doing this new gig-share thing?' Ruth ventured as Nova wrestled to push her backpack under the seat in front of her.

'Nope,' she said, 'but as you know, faux-folk mainstream fare isn't exactly my bag, so . . .'

Her friends were quiet, and she stopped messing with her bag. 'What?'

Gemma cleared her throat. 'It's no biggie, but . . . Well, apparently Flightpath are now playing tomorrow instead, as some sort of fuel-saving green initiative? Something to do with where all the bands and their crew are . . .'

Nova sat back in her seat. 'Great.'

Tiegen leaned across her girlfriend to reach a reassuring hand over, touching Nova's arm. 'It doesn't mean anything. Like, even if Sam is there, you can just ignore him, right?'

Nova patted her friend's hand, and nodded as the coach set off. 'Definitely.' *Definitely* would make it a hundred per cent more difficult not to worry about bumping into Sam in every crowd! 'No worries.' *Many worries*, she thought to herself.

'Gem, why have you packed hair straighteners?' Nova asked, chuckling as they unpacked their stuff. 'Your hair is too short, and there isn't even anywhere to plug . . . Oh wow, there actually *is* electricity in here!'

'Hah!' Gemma said smugly. 'And they're mini

ones. You never know when I might want to go for a straighter, Halle Berry look . . .'

Gem had insisted that Nova share her deluxe yurt instead of setting up a tent, and Nova was stunned to see two low beds made up with sheets and a duvet, little night stands, a mirror, sheepskin rugs on the floor, and lockable cupboards! Not to mention the fact that there were very clean, very posh toilets and showers in the glamping enclosure, too! It was a far cry from what Nova was used to at festivals, and she was relishing the luxury of it all. At first she had teased Gem about bringing her wheely suitcase again, but actually it was Nova who was beginning to feel a bit out of place with her dusty backpack stuffed with clothes!

'Right, Hannah Eagle is playing on the Top Pop stage in fifteen minutes,' Gemma said, looking at her phone. 'T and Ruth are saying something about everyone heading there to be ironic or whatever . . .'

'Ugh,' Nova retorted, but she supposed she had to be a team player for this festival. When she could, she fully planned to drag Gem off to see some of the more left-field performers on the smaller stages. She allowed her bestie to snap off a few selfies of them outside the yurt before they went to meet their friends, battling through the excited crowds on the first day of Berks Beats. It was one of the most popular festivals with a younger audience, and the GCSE results coinciding with the festival made it all the more heaving with teenagers. Nova tried not to scan each tall, tanned boy anxiously as though she might run into Sam at any moment, but so far she was failing.

Just enjoy yourself, she repeated over and again in her mind.

After a lot of shouting into their mobiles over the pounding music around them, Nova and Gemma managed to find their group, though Nova's heart sank a little as she saw the boys arrive. She was happy to see Clive, Tyrell, Mike and some of their other mates, but she definitely could have done without Nate being there. Nova shook it off, and even managed to get swept up with her friends' loud singing along to Hannah Eagle's radio-friendly hits, dancing and laughing. She had to admit she was pretty impressed with the stage show the young singer put on.

After the set finished, everyone was sweaty, hungry and thirsty, so the group made their way to a hot dog stand. The overpriced, lack-lustre food did make Nova nostalgic for her parents' delicious, sustainable truck, and she remembered to fire off a message to assure them she was fine. She and her friends found a clearing on the rapidly browning grass nearby to eat their food, and Nova was once again grateful for Gemma's over-preparedness as her friend shook out her fancy throw-rug to lay on the ground. She, Gem, Tiegen and Ruth spread out on it, and Nova tried to swallow down her jealousy, watching Ruth and T snuggling up together after they finished eating, kissing and giggling. *One* day, she really hoped to find a romantic interest that wouldn't break her heart . . .

'OK, Connie Constance is playing on the

Discovery stage in a few, hon – time for some decent music, eh?' Nova said, grinning at Gem. 'We can leave these two lovebirds to it.'

Gemma nodded, giving Nova a knowing look and pulling her up to her feet. She dusted off her extra-cute Ankara-patterned playsuit and linked arms with Nova. They spent the afternoon watching a few of the performances on the Discovery stage, then choking with laughter after finding a stall selling novelty hats, trying lots of them on and photographing each other. Gemma insisted on buying each of them diamanté-embellished baseball caps that said 'My Best Friend is Sooo Extra'! Nova lost the battle for having the pictures they took posted on Gemma's social media, but at least, she realised, she hadn't thought about Sam in . . . Well, maybe an hour? Progress!

As the evening drew closer, Nova and Gemma met back up with their friends, and Nova felt a wash of relief that they'd decided to skip the first night headliners – she would definitely have had to cry off going to see Flightpath play, ironically or

367

not! Instead, they got more food and took it back to the glamping site, where they managed to dominate an area that had a fire pit surrounded by outdoor beanbags. The night was warm, and lounging on a brightly coloured bag, Nova felt happier than she had in a while as she bantered with her mates. Maybe heading back to school for her A levels wouldn't be so bad after all? Gemma was braiding Ruth's loosely curled hair into two fat cornrows. Tiegen had somehow come across an abandoned ukulele and was strumming it.

'This is like a guitar for a three-year-old,' she said with a chuckle, but still managed to pick out the chords to a Bob Marley song. Almost without thinking, Nova began to hum, then sing along. She realised her friends had all stopped talking to listen, and raised her voice, beginning to belt out the song while Tiegen played. When they finished, even other people from the campsite gave a round of applause.

'Wow!' Ruth said, her eyes wide. 'Since when do you sing like that, Nova?'

'Mate, she always has,' Gemma interjected. 'I've been telling you, Nov – you're amazing!'

Tiegen was nodding enthusiastically. 'Like, next level good!'

'She writes her own songs, too! That's where her real magic is!' Gemma was saying, and Nova fought the urge to shake it off, or to cringe.

'Yeah, I do a bit,' she said softly. Even if her grades meant she was on a path to her environmental science plans, she'd decided something to herself. There was no harm keeping her singer-songwriter dreams alive alongside it. Maybe . . . She hated to credit him with anything, but Nova realised that maybe Sam had helped her discover she didn't need to hide that side of herself. She sighed, and noticed her friends had too, but for different reasons.

'Awright?'

Clive, Nate and some of the boys had turned up by the campfire. They promptly began laughing and punching each other rowdily.

'Ugh, this is why I'm dating an older guy!'

Gemma said, watching as the boys got into an increasingly raucous play-fight. 'Watch it, you lot!' she shouted, as they tussled closer to the fire.

'Apparently Fred Fergusson managed to sneak in some beers,' Nova said to her friend, shaking her head.

Nate, in particular, seemed to be having difficulty standing up straight as they finally stopped with their punch-a-thon, still laughing at one another loudly. She was glad she had already messaged her parents to let them know she was OK – not that she had any intention of getting involved in their silliness. She remembered Gem's 'older guy' comment, and smiled.

'By the way, hon, Otis is hardly a beacon of maturity, either, Gem – be prepared. You should see him with that stupid gaming headset on.'

Gemma got a dreamy expression on her face, and Nova regretted bringing her brother up. 'I've been playing him at *Kick Kombat* online, actually,' she informed Nova.

'Wow, you truly *must* be smitten,' she said,

chuckling at Gemma. 'And, I assume, you guilted your dad into buying you a console?'

Gemma shrugged, an amused look on her face. 'Wouldn't necessarily say *guilted* . . .'

Nova patted her knee, feeling bad at her choice of words. 'I know, babe. Well, look, it will all be worth it to see you kick Otis' butt at that game in a month or so. I can't wait to see his face!'

'To be fair, I have already surprised myself with how— Can I help you?' Gemma cut off, addressing someone behind Nova. She turned around and saw Nathan standing over her beanbag, swaying slightly.

'Nova . . . Can I talk to you?' he said, his voice sounding slurred.

Nova sighed. 'Nate, I think what you should do is drink a litre of water and take yourself to bed,' she said. But he ignored her, squatting down beside her.

'I'd suggest you take her advice,' Gemma said, sitting up a little, but Nate was already speaking.

'Nov, please . . . I seriously messed up by

splitting up with you,' he said, slurring slightly. 'I'm really in to you and I know you still fancy me, too—'

'Nate, give it a rest. I'm not interested,' Nova said firmly, but Nate lurched awkwardly towards her, trying to press his lips to hers. She pushed him on the shoulder, and he tumbled backwards, his limbs flailing. Nova stood up, feeling upset that their evening was descending into drama. She felt Gemma at her side.

'You all right?' her friend said, touching Nova's arm. She nodded, watching as Nate stumbled to standing again.

'Tell me you're not interested?' he said, frowning as he dusted himself unsteadily.

'Pretty sure I already did,' Nova said, folding her arms. She could feel their friends watching the interaction now, and wished she could just head into the yurt away from them all.

'No way you don't want this,' Nate said, gesturing up and down at himself. 'You were practically begging me not to dump you before.'

Nova heard Gemma scoff at his side, but her voice was laced with warning. 'Goodbye, Nate.'

As he turned around, Nova was pretty sure Nate muttered something rude about her under his breath. She wanted to shout at him to say it with his chest, but just then, a tall, familiar figure stepped out of the darkness.

CHAPTER 26

'What'd you just say?'

Nova felt betrayed by her stupid heart and the way it leapt at the mere sight of Sam in the flickering firelight. He was frowning as he squared off with Nate.

'*What'd you just say*?' Nate mocked, doing a bad approximation of Sam's American accent. 'Who's this idiot?' he asked towards his friends.

'Mate, leave it,' Clive ventured, but it was half-hearted at best. Everyone had begun to gather round, watching the two boys.

Nate got in Sam's face. 'I don't have to repeat

myself for you, Yankee boy. Stay out of this, it's nothing to do with you.'

'Back it up,' Sam said, one finger pushing at the centre of Nate's chest. 'Nova is my business.'

Another rush of pleasure filled Nova's spirit at that, but it was quickly dampened as she looked at the two boys. Nate raised both his hands, shoving Sam, who took one step backwards, then retaliated, rushing forwards with his palms outstretched. He made contact with Nate, but Nova's ex seemed prepared, grappling with Sam while the other boys started to shout in excitement about the escalating fight.

'Oi!' Nova shouted, rushing towards them. 'Stop it!'

'Allow it, you two!' Gemma also hollered, right beside Nova, ready to back her up.

Finally, one of Nate's friends intervened, pulling him away as he still struggled to get to Sam.

'*Both* of you are acting ridiculous,' Nova said to them, trembling a little with anger and hurt – or was it the sight of seeing Sam again? As she looked at him, he blew out a long stream of air, straightening his T-shirt.

'Nova, I'm sorry. I just wanted to talk, but this—'

She shook her head and held up a hand. 'Sam . . .' It still hurt to say that name, and to look into those big, green eyes sparkling earnestly in the moonlight. But she held strong. 'Trust me, I do not need rescuing. Just go, OK?'

Sam's shoulders slumped noticeably, but he held up his hands. 'All right. I just . . .' He pulled something from his back pocket. 'I wanted to give you this.' It was a folded piece of paper, which Nova took reluctantly, hoping doing so quickly would stop everyone staring at them. She was relieved as she saw the boys from her school stumbling away to their own campsite. Sam looked down at her a moment longer, and then turned, shoving his hands in his jeans pockets as he walked dejectedly away.

'Phew,' Gemma said, linking her arm into Nova's. 'I mean, feminism first and all, but having two fit guys fighting over you has to be something of an ego boost,' she said with a smile.

Nova returned it half-heartedly, and they said goodbye to their other friends, definitely deciding they should call it a night. After using the fancy bathrooms, she and Gemma settled into their yurt, and soon Nova heard her friend snoring softly.

In spite of the far more comfortable camping arrangements, Nova couldn't sleep. She'd been willing herself not to look at the note that Sam had given her, but eventually she couldn't resist any longer. Using the light from her phone, she unfolded it, and scanned the words that Sam had written.

Nova,

I wrote this down in case you didn't want to talk, which if I've given this to you I guess is true, and I totally understand. I never, ever meant to hurt you, and I cannot tell you how sorry I am. It was unbelievably dumb of me to go on to autopilot and not tell you about my dad, about my name, about everything. But you know the <u>essence</u> of me, I promise you. And also, you have my heart, if it's OK for me to tell you that . . .

Being so mad at my dad about how things were back when I was a kid made me too defensive, too quick to worry about other people's reactions. Now that he's clean, and this huge star, it's like nobody knows or cares the hard stuff we've gone through. The stuff I opened up to you about, I hardly ever tell anyone. It's weird — I read his book, and it really made me know how much regret he has, how hard he's trying to make it right now. You told me to let him do that, and I've started to finally listen to your advice. And of course, you were right.

I trust you, Nova, and it kills me that you feel I've broken your trust in me.

I want to make it up to you. I'll do whatever I can to make this right, but if I can't, know that this has been the most special

summer ever for me. I just can't believe I
messed it up so bad.

I shouldn't be asking for you to forgive me,
but I thought I'd give it one last shot.

Sam xx

Nova stared at the letter, reading it over and
again, running a finger over the way he'd signed it
off, underlining his name. Could she forgive him?

Suddenly something hit Nova, and in the
darkness of the yurt, she felt around for her jeans
and a hoodie, then quietly tiptoed out of the tent.
She'd brought one more thing – her Dictaphone.
Sitting in one of the beanbags next to the dying
embers of the campfire, she began to sing softly
into it . . .

Nova stirred from sleep as she felt the mattress of
her bed shift, followed by the sound of a camera,
and a bright flash that she perceived even through

her closed eyelids.

'I'm posting that in ten seconds if you don't wake up!'

Nova blinked awake, and saw Gemma looming over her, grinning. She pulled herself up to sitting, and reached for her own phone – it was already ten in the morning. 'Sorry, babe,' she said, yawning. 'I didn't get to sleep for a while last night.'

Gemma gave her a knowing look. 'I'm aware – pretty sure I heard your dulcet tones in the night, or was that a dream? Were you writing something?'

Nova nodded. 'Yeah, I kind of felt inspired all of a sudden.'

Gemma patted her arm. 'That's fantastic, Nov! Let that muse move you, eh!'

Nova chuckled, swinging her feet out of the bed and sitting beside Gemma. She stretched and stood up. Her face grew more serious as she looked down at her friend. 'Actually, I was thinking about all the stuff with Sam. Don't judge me, but—'

'One step ahead of you, hon. He's forgiven?'

Nova nodded.

'OK. Judgement-free zone. I mean, I'm a claimed woman and I'd never be interested in my mate's man, but are you mad? Sam's gorgeous, talented and a complete sweetheart. So he was a bit liberal with the truth? So what?'

Nova pulled a face. 'Yeah. I was just hurt, and after all the stuff with Nate . . .' She tailed off as Gem held up a palm.

'Don't speak that legit moron's name, hon.' She stood up so she was eye to eye with Nova. 'You can make things work with Sam, I know you can.'

'How, though?'

Gemma tapped the side of her temple like a real-life meme. 'Your girl has the knowledge, trust me. But first, we need to deal with that morning breath . . .' She grimaced, and Nova reached out to tickle her, but then pulled her friend into a hug.

'Thanks, babe,' she said, squeezing her. 'Off to the showers I go, then.'

Half an hour later, feeling a bit fresher, Nova zipped up her black denim shorts and peered outside, deciding to throw a loose oversized cardigan over her blue cami-top, just in case. She headed out of the yurt to where Gemma was video chatting with Otis, holding up a page of the novel she was reading.

'This bit was amaaaazing,' she was saying, and Nova could see her brother's face grinning on her friend's screen.

'Yeah, thought you'd like that scene,' he replied. It was cute – if also a bit eww – the way they were sharing their favourite books and stuff. Nova squatted down so that Gemma's camera could pick her up, too.

'You two are soooo adorable,' she said, and Otis gave her a good-natured but rude gesture.

'See you soon, boo,' Gemma said, and Otis winked.

'Bye, baby.'

Nova stifled an 'ugh' as Gemma signed off.

'Right. I need to tell you something,' her friend said, then paused ominously. 'Don't be angry but—'

'Gem!'

'I said *don't* be angry!'

'I'm not. Go on, spit it out!'

Gemma laughed and held up her phone. 'So, I might have stayed friends with Sam on Insta. Disloyal, but important, I reckon – I had to monitor the situation and that.'

Nova raised an eyebrow. 'Right . . .'

'Well, your bestie might have seen something interesting on his feed . . .'

Nova's heart sank. Did he go off and hook up with some groupie when she rejected him last night? 'Oh, listen, if it's bad—'

Gemma shook her head vigorously. 'Nope. But he is playing a full-on, proper slot on the Discovery stage! And it's in . . .' She looked at her phone's time display. 'Oops. Five minutes.' She stood up and grabbed Nova's hand. 'We need to get our skates on because you, my dear friend, are about to go and get your man back!'

CHAPTER 27

The crowds were unbearable as Nova gripped Gemma's hand tightly, trying not to get separated as they rushed across the Berks Beats site towards the Discovery stage. The sun was already high in the sky, and Nova had to get Gem to stop so that she could tie her cardi around her waist. Her feet were hot in her Doc Marten boots, and by the time they were in sight of the stage, they were at least ten minutes past Sam's start time. Nova felt sweaty and scared and in no way ready to confront him and try and reconcile things, and now they'd have to wait until after his set.

'Wow, I know your boy is getting popular online, but this is crazy!' Gemma called to Nova, as they elbowed their way towards the front. But they soon realised why the crowds were so dense there. The giant video screen behind the stage showed a very recognisable figure waving as he strode on to the stage carrying a guitar. Sam was already at a microphone, and smiled towards the man joining him.

'All right, so . . . This is kind of crazy, but we've never done this before. Ladies and gentlemen, my *father . . .*' He paused, emphasising the word as a palpable ripple swept through the audience at this news. 'The incredible Mr Clay Cooper!'

The audience burst into applause, and Nova stared up at the stage, pulling Gemma to a halt. 'Wow,' she breathed, and Gem grinned at her.

'Let's try and get closer to the front!' she shouted over the whoops and cheers.

As Nova and her friend elbowed their way towards the stage, she heard Clay say, 'Nice one, son!' He reached over and gave Sam a tight hug while a roadie – an *actual* roadie – rushed on to the stage to place a couple of stands with microphones next to Sam's. 'Ladies and gents, is my boy not incredible himself?' Clay said into one of them. The crowd cheered their assent. 'I'm so proud, Yo, I can't tell ya.'

Nova paused from making her way through the hot, heaving bodies to glance up at Sam's dad beaming and looking a little tearful. He strummed his acoustic guitar to check the tuning, and angled the microphones towards himself more.

'Thanks, Pop.' Sam's voice boomed over the speakers. 'What do you say we do one of your numbers? I hear they're pretty popular.'

As Nova and Gemma finally reached the barriers at the front of the crowd, they heard the two men launch into a stripped back, really beautiful duet of one of Flightpath's earlier songs. As they concluded in a close harmony, Nova felt tears prickle her own eyes – the two of them sounded wonderful singing together! They hugged tightly again, and Clay waved as he left the stage to rapturous cheering. Sam adjusted his guitar, then reached down and took a sip of water from the bottle at his feet, as though he needed a moment to compose himself.

'I think that guy has a future,' he quipped as he stood up again. 'Catch him again on the Main Stage a little later, I hear ...' His cheeky grin slackened as he looked down at the crowd. Nova turned to her side and saw Gemma gesticulating wildly up at him.

'Gem, what are you doing?' she said through a clenched smile, pulling her friend's arms down.

'Uh ... Sorry, folks, I just spotted a friend of mine,' Sam said into the mic. Gemma shook her hands free, cupped her hands around her mouth and shouted, 'She needs to talk to you!'

'Gem!' Nova exclaimed. 'Now is, like, the complete opposite of the right time—'

Sam smiled down at them. 'How would you guys feel about another guest right now? I mean, I know I'm sharing the stage here kind of a lot for my first official gig, but ... Did you guys check out the video I posted with a young lady by the name of Nova Clarke?'

To Nova's surprise, a ripple of applause swept around the audience, and even a couple of whoops.

'What do you say I get her up here to sing with me again?'

Nova felt her heart in her throat, but Sam's eyes bored directly down into hers, and something clicked. She sucked in the deepest breath, and no longer felt afraid. A festival steward helped her over the metal barrier that was set a few feet back from the stage, and Sam reached down a hand to help her up – thankfully it wasn't too high, because for a flicker of a moment Nova worried about an inelegant pic of her clambering up a stage ending up online, but she shook that off, too, and found herself pressed against Sam's warm body as he pulled her up towards him.

'Hey,' he breathed.

'Hey,' she replied, grinning up into his beautiful face. 'Th-thanks for your letter.' It was almost like they had forgotten a huge crowd was watching them, until Nova became aware of the clapping and cheering. She glanced out to the audience, and her head swam with nerves again, but only for a moment. She turned back to Sam, then stepped towards his microphone as he hung back, still looking a bit dazed that she was there.

'Hi, guys,' she began, then cleared her throat. 'Actually, I wondered if I could sing you something of my own really quickly.' She felt Sam at her side, and addressed her last comment to him. He nodded enthusiastically.

Nova heard herself breathing shakily into the mic over the speaker system, but she opened her mouth to begin the song she'd written the night before. It was just her voice, a capella, loud and clear, soulful and jazzy, and the crowd settled into a hush as she sang.

The lyrics were among the most personal she'd ever written, but she squeezed her eyes shut and sang her heart out, taking her short song a key higher as she hit the final refrain.

'*I know what we had was true,*

And I want you to know, I forgive you.'

She finished, holding the last, lingering note before panting as she stepped back from the mic.

Wait, did that just actually happen? she thought to herself. The crowd was silent. But then a huge wave of shouts, cheers and applause engulfed her, and she stared out at the audience, and then over to Sam. He looked shocked, thrilled, and most of all, proud. He rushed over, pushing his guitar on to his back, and swept her into a tight hug, pulling her up and spinning her around before his lips covered hers, warm and urgent.

When he finally broke away, he shouted into the microphone. 'This is my girlfriend, guys. How lucky am I? Wow!' The crowd cheered again, and Sam began to strum the opening chords to the song they'd written together. 'I'm hoping she won't mind singing this one with me, too . . .'

Together they launched into the song, sharing Sam's microphone and singing their hearts out. Nova felt like her heart really was out – out in the open for everyone to see as she stared at Sam's handsome face while he belted out their song. She felt endless possibility.

She could do this, whenever she was ready to. She could share her music – and her heart.

'Nah, you don't understand, let me in! I'm her best mate...!' Nova heard Gemma's voice insistently shouting. Her pulse was still pounding from what had happened out there as Sam pulled her backstage.

'Let her through, guys,' Sam called towards the security, still clutching tightly to Nova's hand. Gemma emitted a squeal only bats could hear as she rushed over to them.

'That! Was! Un! Believable!' Gemma cried, practically suffocating Nova with her hug, then turning to squeeze Sam into one, too. 'Nov, I... I'm speechless!'

Nova grinned at her friend. 'Thanks so much, Gem. You always have my back.'

'Well, if your brother puts a ring on it, we'll be sisters for real,' she said, winking.

'Let's not get ahead of ourselves . . .'

She felt Sam's hand on the small of her back again.

'Nova?' he said. 'I'd like you to meet my dad.' She turned to see a smiling Clay Cooper. He too pulled Nova into a hug.

'You have got some vocals on you, young lady,' he said, clutching her shoulders for a moment before letting go. 'I can definitely understand why Yo here is smitten with you . . . Err, Sam, I mean,' he corrected himself.

'It's OK, Dad,' Sam said softly, before turning back to Nova. 'I'm smitten for real though, can't deny it.' He kissed Nova briefly, and she blushed.

'It's really good to meet you, Mr Cooper,' she said.

'Please, it's Clay. You've made my boy really happy, Nova. Can't thank you enough.' He rubbed her shoulder again, said a quick hello to Gemma, and then waved to someone else in the backstage area. 'See you in a bit, yeah?'

While Gemma proceeded to message every single one of their friends with a video of what had just happened, telling them that they just missed the greatest musical moment of all time, Sam pulled Nova into a quiet area outside behind the stage.

'So . . . Did you mean what you sang up there?'

'Every word,' Nova said, feeling shy now as Sam trailed his fingers up her bare arms, leaving goosebumps in their wake.

'You forgive me?'

'Yes,' she said quietly. 'Do *you* forgive *me*?'

He leaned down closer to her. 'Nothing to forgive,' he whispered, before his mouth met hers. Nova sighed, feeling tears prickle her eyes as he pulled away from the kiss.

'What are we going to do when you go back, though?' she asked sadly.

To her slight confusion, Sam shrugged as he said, 'Well, it'll only be for a couple weeks.'

She frowned. 'What do you mean?'

'I'll head back to Miami, grab my stuff, see

Mom and Teo . . . They'll come over here in a couple months to visit as well, so—'

'Wait . . . You . . .'

'Got in to London College of Music? Yup.'

'And you're . . .'

'Going to come study here? Yup.'

Nova let out a squeal that rivalled Gemma's, then leapt into Sam's arms. He held her close, laughing and rubbing her back as he supported her weight with zero effort. 'I'm going to be right back here with you before you know it, Nova Clarke. Can't get rid of me that easy,' he said, his low voice rumbling through her body. She slackened her grip and he lowered her to the ground. 'We've got some music to make,' he said.

She smiled. 'Yeah. I think we do.'